Leftovers

Leftovers

04341077087-8

HEATHER WALDORF

ORCA BOOK PUBLISHERS

Library and Archives Canada Cataloguing in Publication

Waldorf, Heather, 1966-
Leftovers / written by Heather Waldorf.

ISBN 978-1-55143-937-2

I. Title.

PS8645.A458L43 2009   jC813'.6   C2008-907663-X

First published in the United States, 2009

Library of Congress Control Number: 2008942003

Summary: An unruly dog and a scrawny teenage cancer survivor help Sarah begin to recover from years of sexual abuse.

Orca Book Publishers gratefully acknowledges the support for its publishing programs provided by the following agencies: the Government of Canada through the Book Publishing Industry Development Program and the Canada Council for the Arts, and the Province of British Columbia through the BC Arts Council and the Book Publishing Tax Credit.

Design by Teresa Bubela
Cover artwork by Getty Images

ORCA BOOK PUBLISHERS
PO Box 5626, STN. B
VICTORIA, BC CANADA
V8R 6S4

ORCA BOOK PUBLISHERS
PO Box 468
CUSTER, WA USA
98240-0468

www.orcabook.com
Printed and bound in Canada.
Printed on 100% PCW recycled paper.

12 11 10 09 • 4 3 2 1

For Ace

ONE

Ah, summer.

Lazy mornings in bed, flipping through back issues of People *and munching on chocolate chip waffles.*

Long afternoons at the beach, slathered in SPF 45 *and sprinkled with sand.*

Breezy nights in the backyard, grilling gourmet veggie dogs under the stars, chilling with some hot guy to Mom's old-dude CDs: *James Taylor, The Eagles, Simon and Garfunkel.*

Worries? None for me, thanks.

Responsibilities? I'll pass.

Rain? Not on my parade.

This is the life. MY life. Me. Sarah Greene. Can you believe it? It's the stuff of prom queens. Of Hollywood daughters. Of romance novel heroines. Of—

BBBBRRRRIIIINNNNGGGG!!!

"I hate you!" I shout at the alarm clock. No way it could be 6:15 AM already. But I've been wrong before. Like yesterday. And the day before that. All week, in fact.

A *way*-too-perky female voice comes over the loud-speaker from the ramshackle lodge across the field. "Good…*SQUAWK*…morning! Out of your…*SQUAWK*…beds, you…*SQUAWK*…sleepyheads! Last…*SQUAWK*…one to the flagpole gets…*SQUAWK, SQUAWK, SQU*—"

Bleary-eyed and yawning, I sit up, whacking my fore-head on the exposed rafters. On my way down from the loft bed, my foot misses the ladder; I tumble from my lumpy mattress to the floor, scraping my elbow. I feel around for the iron bedpost and pull myself to my feet, fighting an overwhelming desire to sprawl on the cool linoleum, maybe catch a few extra zzzzz's.

"Crap," I mumble, wincing at my lemon-sucking reflec-tion in the mini-mirror nailed to the wall.

Pulling on the first musty pieces of clothing I find scattered around the drafty cabin (cabin is way overstating it; my quarters are no bigger than a glorified garden shed), I run a four-foot mad dash into my "private" bathroom, which is a closet containing a toilet, a sink and a shower stall as narrow as an upright coffin. I slap a Band-Aid on my scraped elbow, brush my teeth and shake out my dusty, peanut-butter-brown bedhead.

Good enough.

At six thirty sharp, I sprint out my cabin door into the early morning fog to join the small stampede across the muddy field to the flagpole.

At Camp Dog Gone Fun, the last one there gets Poo Patrol.

TWO

I make it to the flagpole second to last. No Poo Patrol for me. Not today. Today I draw the Grooming straw. Forget my own grooming; for three leisurely hours this morning, I'll be washing, drying, fluffing and brushing out the matted and dirt-encrusted coats of a dozen-odd dogs of questionable parentage.

Not that my own parentage is anything to brag about.

Case in point: "Camp God Damn *what?*" my mother asked a month ago when she found out where they were sending me—"they" being the fine folks who run the juvenile court system.

Here's the truth: There are worse places to spend a summer. Like a detention home for girls voted most likely to kill their families with an ax. Or a Britney Spears fan convention. Or one of those places where you chant, eat tofu and do yoga three times a day.

Camp Dog Gone Fun isn't one of those ridiculous rich-doggie spas that you see in magazines either. There are no canine treadmills or therapy baths. No animal masseuse or pet psychic is on call. Bottom line, all the canine campers at Camp Dog Gone Fun are rejects from the River View Animal Shelter in Gananoque, Ontario. Dogs who, because of old age or disability or "quirky" behavioral issues, are impossible to adopt out. Each summer, the program director—a veterinarian everyone calls Dr. Fred (even his wife)—ferries the dogs here to Moose Island on the St. Lawrence River for a "wilderness" respite from the shelter. He can't afford to hire real staff, so he brings over a bunch of community service kids too and calls us "volunteers."

So when exactly did my life, as we say here at Camp Dog Gone Fun, go to the dogs?

At my sentencing, the judge told me that Camp DGF is where "kids like you" are sent.

I whispered to my lawyer, "Kids who lick their behinds and howl at the moon?"

"No, young lady," the judge, who'd overheard me, shot back. "I was referring to kids who lack any real criminal intent but whose impulsive actions have resulted in trouble with the law. Kids who might benefit from the fresh air, physical activity and team spirit at the camp. Kids who might actually welcome the opportunity to complete all of their community service hours over a two-month summer period instead of having to juggle them with homework, part-time jobs and family responsibilities during the school year. Kids who—"

Whatever, already. I was happy to go. Really. Anything to get away from the question on everyone's lips.

"Why, Sarah?" the police had asked. "Why did you do it? Is there trouble at home?"

Nope, I thought, shaking my head. Not since Dad bit the bullet. Or, more accurately, the filet mignon.

"Why, Sarah?" asked all the outwardly concerned, inwardly titillated kids at school. The fact that my "impulsive actions" were the most exciting gossip to orbit the cafeteria since Jake Miller sliced off his big toe on a lawnmower blade the previous summer shows how starved some small-town kids are for real excitement. I responded to their nosy inquiries with lava-freezing glares and middle-finger salutes.

"Why, Sarah?" asked my mother. "Are you upset that I've started dating again?"

Like I care. My mother could date the mailman, Tom Cruise or the rottweiler next door, and I wouldn't bat an eyelash.

Too bad, really. It would be such an easy out to blame my mother's boyfriend, Tanner, for my "impulsive actions." But all he's truly guilty of is bad clothes sense and pointing the digital Nikon camera he won in a work raffle at my face. "Say cheese," he'd said, grinning.

I was at the kitchen table, studying for a biology test. "Piss off," I snarled. And I was serious. Serious as cancer. Already the kitchen was morphing into a poorly maintained carnival ride. The floor spun in time with the ceiling fan, and my chair legs turned to rubber. My chest pounded out an angry heavy-metal anthem. I'd swear the two-dimensional frog guts in my bio book began twitching.

But Tanner just laughed and kept fiddling with the camera.

"For God's sake, Sarah," my mother said from across the room where she was fixing coffee. "Just smile, for crying out loud."

Without thinking—barely breathing—I slammed my ten-pound textbook closed and pitched it at Tanner's face, knocking his camera to the floor, where it smashed to smithereens on the ceramic tiles. I bolted out of my chair and grabbed Tanner's car keys off the counter. Ignoring Tanner's shocked expression and my mother's angry shouts, I fled out the side door.

THREE

"I just had to get out of there" was how I'd explained it to my mother at the police station, after a trip to the hospital. Forget that I was still only fifteen, obviously had no license, and my only driving experience was behind the wheel of a golf cart last fall in my cousin's apple orchard. Not too surprising that I'd totaled the car.

"You'll have to get over this ridiculous picture-taking phobia one day, Sarah," she said. "I'd understand if you were deformed or overweight, but you're an attractive young woman—when you aren't scowling. You cut school on picture days. You won't sit for family portraits. You destroyed Tanner's new camera." She buried her head in her hands and mumbled through her fingers. "This is crazy. *Crazy*."

I shrugged. Best to let her assume that my phobia came from low self-esteem. Also best to let her assume that all that Polaroid film charged to my father's Visa over the years was used to snap quick pictures for his recipe portfolio.

It's true that he did that sometimes. My father had dreamed of writing a cookbook some day. In fact, he'd been in Montreal last summer, at a lunch meeting with a potential publisher, when he choked—rhymes with croaked—on a piece of steak.

It was the best day of my life, if you consider what all my previous days had been like. Grief is a strong emotion, but so is relief.

Tanner came over and handed me a can of Coke and my mother a cup of vending-machine coffee. I didn't get why he was there. He'd been at the hospital too. He even seemed relieved when I'd been discharged with a clean bill of health.

What was in it for him? Did he really love my mother? Nah. He probably just thought I'd done him a favor. His insurance would probably buy him a much nicer car than the shitbox I'd totaled.

Mom took a sip of her coffee, winced and then tried a different tactic with me. "Dad and I used to love taking pictures of you when you were a toddler. We have albums full of you."

I hate it when my mother refers to her late husband as "Dad." I hate that he was my dad. In junior high, I used to fantasize that I'd been the result of some lurid one-night stand between my mother and a South American rock musician. I imagined my real father was a drummer (or maybe a bass player) named Marcos (or maybe Juan), who blew through town for one hot night of passion and never came back. It didn't bother me that Marcos/Juan had never tried to make contact with me. He probably didn't even know I existed. There are worse things than being ignored. Trust me.

"What about your graduation next year?" Mom blathered on. "Or your wedding? What if you have your own children some day? Will you never take pictures of them?"

I gulped. "Never."

"Fine," my mother said, crossing her arms in defeat. "But Sarah, someday you'll be sorry that you have no photos. You can't always rely on your memory…"

Ha. Joke's on her. I have plenty of photos to look at. All I need is one more chance to find them. I'd bungled my first attempt horribly, but I can't let that—let anything or any*one*—stop me.

Finding those photos was—and still is—my mission in life.

A search-and-destroy mission.

Nothing else matters.

FOUR

Sweaty under the midmorning sun, covered in wet dog hair, my hands smelling of tar shampoo and oatmeal conditioner, I call a break and pass out Milkbones to my charges. These old, disabled, quirky dogs wag their tails like crazy. They love me—love anybody who brushes them and gives them affection and biscuits. Especially biscuits.

Here's the truth: I don't mind them either. The dogs never gawk at me or peer over the rims of their eyeglasses and coffee mugs like my teachers, neighbors and even my boss down at the Doughy Donut Emporium, question marks flashing in their eyes. The dogs never say things like:

"Sarah's usually so responsible. Intelligent. Not reckless at all! Wasn't she lucky to have survived the crash?"

"Yes, Ian's death must have been hard on her, but it's been almost a year now. Her marks haven't suffered. So what happened?"

"It's always the quiet ones you have to watch out for, isn't it?"

And the dogs don't gather in the high school cafeteria either, like my classmates back home, whispering about my so-called accident behind my back.

"*Sarah's such a freeeeeeeak!*"

"*So Sarah doesn't like her mother's new boyfriend. That's no reason to steal his car, is it? She hasn't even finished driver's ed!*"

"*OMG!!! Is it true that Sarah raced down Commerce Street like she had the cops on her ass?*"

MORONS, all of them.

Remember that old *Sesame Street* song, "Who Are the People in Your Neighborhood?" I don't know about the people in *other* neighborhoods, but the people in *my* neighborhood are idiots. Or, as we say here at Camp Dog Gone Fun, barking up the wrong tree.

Because no one ever asked *where* I was going that night.

Good thing too.

FIVE

The only other thing you might be interested to know about my "neighborhood"—Riverwood, Ontario, population 3,700—is that it's a sleepy rural community of hobby farmers, Ottawa commuters and their families, and a handful of assorted oddballs. And that it looked even sleepier while I was careening down the main drag in a stolen car on that foggy, fateful night last March, hell-bent on reaching the highway that would take me an hour's drive northeast to the city of Ottawa. To my dead father's restaurant.

Tanner's car was in fast-forward that night, but I saw only still shots out the windshield. Garth Brooks was singing on the radio, but I heard only sound effects worthy of some cheesy Hollywood action flick. Some highlights:

SWOOSH! St. Bart's United Church. The place is packed with women each Sunday. And it's not because the town's females are all seriously into the God thing. It's because Reverend Donaldson is single *and* a dead ringer for Matthew McConaughey. Even the blue-haired choir ladies jockey for the chair closest to the pulpit.

VRRROOOOMMM! Old Man Kevert's body shop. Mr. Kevert is Riverwood's one-man freak show. He brags about keeping a two-headed baby raccoon in a jar of formaldehyde in his refrigerator. Mr. Kevert doesn't give out candy at Halloween; instead he shows kids his "trick," which involves popping out his glass eyeball and rattling his false teeth and nobody knows what else because kids generally take off down the street screaming at that point.

ROARRRR! Jeff Grenville, the star of Riverwood High's concert band, was slouched against the Coke machine in front of Alvin's Arcade, eyeing my Paul Tracy impersonation with—was that curiosity? Concern? No, more like envy.

BEEEEP! I waved and blasted the horn at him just for fun, knowing there wasn't much chance he'd recognized me through the unfamiliar windshield and the after-dinner darkness.

ZOOOOM! Over the bridge. Melvin's Grill to the left. Phil's Pharmacy to the right. I've always thought that the two places should get together and offer some sort of promotion: buy two grease-burgers for lunch and get a free frothy pink Pepto-Bismol shake to go. I was glad I'd eaten supper before escaping in Tanner's car. As fast as I was driving, it would still take a while to get where I was going and do the nasty but necessary job that needed to be done. I hadn't exactly thought to bring a snack.

A white streak of fur darted in front of Tanner's car. Fluffbucket. He belongs to Ms. Jeppsie, my math teacher. What I want to know is, if felines are so smart, why don't they look both ways before they cross the street? Then again, Fluffbucket is *old*, eighteen or nineteen, and in all those cat-years he'd never known Commerce Street to be a particularly hazardous roadway. Until that night, Riverwood was a town where people stuck to the speed limit and obeyed the *Slow. Watch for Children* signs, extending the same courtesy to cats, dogs, squirrels and even the occasional skunk.

SCREEEEEEEEEEEECH! I slammed my foot down on the brake pedal, swerved to the left and lost control of Tanner's rusty red Neon, a car which, under normal circumstances, I wouldn't be caught dead driving. If I actually knew how to drive.

Clenching my eyes shut didn't help matters any. But when the concrete likeness of Harold Medeler, World War One fighter pilot, standing at attention atop the town war memorial as proudly as a plastic groom on a wedding cake, comes straight at you at eighty-odd kilometers per hour, the less you can see the better.

At the moment of impact, all I heard was an ear-splitting *CRACK*, which I assumed was my head going through the windshield. It turned out to be the front bumper against the cenotaph, and Harold's head flying through the Neon's front window into the passenger seat.

Then the *WHOOSH* of the airbag.

Then the sirens.

Obviously I survived (so did Fluffbucket) despite what I've heard about the left-hander's tendency toward poor hand-foot-eye coordination and the increased probability of dying in a motor-vehicle accident. Harold was rescued and sent to the city cement works to have his head reattached. He was back at his post a week later. Tanner's car was a write-off.

That I could have killed old Fluffbucket, who has been in the world longer than I have, makes me cringe, and thank God, or Matthew McConaughey, that he had at least one of his nine lives left. That I could have killed a child or someone's grandma out for her nightly stroll was something new to lose sleep about. That I had defaced—accidentally, but *literally*—the only real monument in town, made me feel as shamed as if I'd shot down Harold's plane in France almost a century ago. That I could have killed myself was beside the point; I had no breaks, no bumps, no scratches even. Then again, I've never bruised or scarred easily.

At least not on the outside.

S I X

At Camp Dog Gone Fun, everyone is too tired and rushed at breakfast to notice or care what Dr. Fred sets out on the table. Which is good, because if you really think about it, facing cold cereal, hard-boiled eggs, canned fruit cocktail and terrible coffee every morning might be the most punishing aspect of life here.

Camp tradition dictates that dinner is prepared by lottery. It's hit or miss depending on who draws the short straw at flagpole and what's on the unimaginative menu sent to Dr. Fred by a dietitian hired by the courts to make sure the "volunteers" aren't fed kibble. Some nights it's spaghetti or hamburgers, which are awfully hard to screw up, even for the kitchen-challenged. But some nights it's tuna casserole or chicken stew, which at best (I don't mean to brag, but when *I* cook) is edible, but at worst (when anyone else cooks) tastes like glue and smells like something the dogs horked up.

But everyone loves lunch. Lunch is always a buffet. A smorgasbord of fruits and veggies and ham and cheese and pickles and nuts.

Not unlike those of us who gather at the big round table to eat it.

At one o'clock sits Dr. Fred, forty-eight, bald as a bowling ball, veterinarian and all-around Mr. Nice Guy.

Two o'clock, Victoria, forty-five, wife of Dr. Fred. A fiery-haired social worker with so much energy she should come with a warning label.

Three o'clock, me. Sarah. Just turned sixteen. As you know, the crash-test dummy of the group.

Four o'clock, Johanna. Also sixteen. A wild-eyed party girl. Last fall, one of her self-described "beer bashes" spilled over to her neighbor's yard. In the morning, a bed of prize-winning Brussels sprouts was dead and an entire family of ceramic lawn gnomes was decapitated. "Oops" was all she had to say about it, punctuated by a toss of her waist-length blond hair.

Five o'clock, Taylor, seventeen. A green-haired artist/poet with enough metal in her face and spikes around her throat to build a motorcycle, and a penchant for spraying pro-choice graffiti on the sides of Catholic churches.

Six, seven, eight *and* nine o'clock, Nicholas, thirteen. Three hundred and sixty-two pounds. Guilty as charged, he admits, of chronic shoplifting to feed his appetite for… well…just about anything.

Ten and eleven o'clock, Brant, seventeen. Mr. Muscles. Star athlete, at least in his own mind. Unlike the rest of us "volunteers," who are from various towns within an hour's drive of the St. Lawrence River, Brant, like Dr. Fred and Victoria, lives just half a mile away, on the mainland in Gananoque. His crime: breaking into a college science lab on a dare and letting out all the mice. His purpose: to impress his vegan, animal activist, now *ex*-girlfriend.

And last but not least, at noon and midnight, sits Sullivan, sixteen. He's from Riverwood, same as me. He's...hey, wait a second. What the hell is Sullivan Vickerson doing at Moose Island? Sullivan wasn't at Camp Dog Gone Fun yesterday. He wasn't even here at breakfast this morning.

Sullivan isn't the best-looking guy or the smartest guy or even the most athletic guy at Riverwood High School. He's actually a short, skinny, somewhat dorky guy who gets called Bozo by some of the meaner kids at school. Mostly because of his enormous feet, which seem clownish attached to his stick legs, and which Sullivan shows off in a vast collection of loudly colored canvas high-tops. I sneak a peek under the table. Today he's wearing a bright yellow pair that conjures up an image of Big Bird.

But Sullivan has something. Maybe it's the Tigger-like bounce in his step as he jaywalks with abandon across the well-worn paths of the jocks, artists and brains, leaving trails through the school drama club, the concert band, the yearbook committee, the cross-country ski club and who knows what else. Sullivan chats up the goths and geeks and gangstas-in-training during lunch hours, volunteers to push the wheelchair kids around on class trips and sells truckloads of chocolate bars for every school fundraising campaign. Even the sourest teachers are known to crack a smile after encountering him. So even if he did find the motivation—or time—to commit an "impulsive action," any judge would take one look at his Colgate grin and let him off scot-free.

So what gives?

"Hi, Sarah," he says, giving me a little wave across the table. I can't remember the last time—or *any* time— that Sullivan has spoken to me directly. I did sometimes catch him gawking at me in English last term, with an odd wrinkle above his left eyebrow like I was some impossibly awkward paragraph he'd been assigned to edit.

"Hey," I reply.

"You two know each other?" Victoria asks.

"Sarah goes to my school," Sullivan replies, grinning as he crunches into a giant dill pickle. Juice dribbles down his chin. He wipes it on his T-shirt sleeve. "She was in my English class last term."

"Sullivan's my son," Victoria explains. "He'll be joining me—joining all of us—again this summer."

My eyes dart from Sullivan to Victoria and back. They don't look much alike. Sullivan is only about five-four— maybe half an inch taller than me—and skinny. His hair is thin and dark brown, spiked on top, probably to make him look taller. Victoria, who is at least five-ten and built as solidly as a pit bull, has thick, fire-engine red curls, whose color, judging by her roots, comes from a box. But yeah, they share the same high cheekbones and bright blue eyes and the seeming inability to sit still for more than ten seconds at a stretch.

Not a chance, though, that Dr. Fred is Sullivan's biological father. And it's not just because Dr. Fred Wong is Chinese. It's because I know that Sullivan's father teaches geography at Riverwood High School. He was my homeroom teacher in ninth grade.

"You're here by court order too?" Brant snorts.

"Yup. Custody arrangement," Sullivan explains. "I live with my dad in Riverwood during the school year and spend summers out here. At Al*dog*traz," he adds, winking at me across the table.

I give my mouth a wrist swipe. Knowing me, the grape juice I slurped moments before has left a purple mustache.

Nicholas laughs out loud, a deep, booming belly-roar that bounces off the walls like a volleyball. "Like Al*cat*raz. The prison, get it?"

"Hi, Sullivan," Johanna says, batting her lashes at him. If I ever tried to pull off a move like that, guys would think I had a facial tic or Tourette's or something.

I spear a cherry tomato with my fork and accidentally elbow Johanna. "Sorry," I mumble. Serves her right for sitting left of a leftie.

Johanna, the drama queen, rubs her arm and—give me a break—inspects it for bruising. "Can we call you Sully?" she asks Sullivan.

"Sully?" Brant guffaws, his mouth full of potato salad.

"Beats a nickname like Bran Flake," I mumble.
Heads swivel toward me. Did I really say that? Out loud?
Sullivan laughs. Loudly. He thinks I've made a joke.
A long summer just got longer.

SEVEN

Every day after lunch, the dogs nap in the shade. There's free time for the "volunteers" until 3:00 PM.

"Enjoy!" Dr. Fred exclaims, opening his arms wide as if to convey that Moose Island is some lush expanse of wilderness. A Canine Club Med. There are no actual moose on Moose Island; it was named for old Richard Moose, a rich, dog-loving bachelor who left the island to Dr. Fred on the condition that it be maintained as a "Pooch Paradise."

Get real.

Here's what Camp DGF *really* looks like:

Imagine a postcard-perfect tropical island in the South Pacific. You know the kind: tall palms swaying gently in the breeze, long stretches of soft sand, a clear green ocean teeming with iridescent fish, fresh air scented with pineapple and coconut, exotic birds soaring and singing across azure skies. In simpler terms: Paradise. Pooch or otherwise.

Then bomb it.

Reduce "Paradise" to a few large boulders and a bucket of rubble. Transport it to eastern Ontario and drop it into the St. Lawrence River, one of the busiest shipping lanes in North America. Plant a few willows and evergreens. Sell it to old Mr. Moose, who hooks up some basic water and electricity and builds a stone lodge, five tiny clapboard guest cabins and a boat launch. Then along comes Dr. Fred, who adds the big modern dog barn.

Look away from the billows of smoke from the factories downstream and the rubbernecking Thousand Islands boat tourists and their expensive video cameras. Don't breathe too deeply, unless you enjoy the stench of fuel and sulfur. Avoid the dead fish that wash up on the briny shore in the wake of the freighters chugging to and from the Atlantic. Swimming? Can you spell *c-o-n-j-u-n-c-t-i-v-i-t-i-s*? And then there are the dogs. Dogs everywhere: big dogs, little dogs, old dogs, three-legged dogs, blind dogs, deaf dogs, confused dogs, nervous, barky, jumpy dogs. (Only the really sick dogs and chronic biters have to stay behind at Dr. Fred's clinic/shelter on the mainland.) So obviously you have to watch where you step.

Things can only get better, right?

That same day, after supper (Victoria made a meatloaf, with more enthusiasm than meat, if you ask me), Dr. Fred pushes back his chair, stands and clears his throat. "A new participant is joining us this evening. It's quite unusual for us to take on a dog once the summer session has started, but, well, this is a special case. You'll see what I mean when—"

"Watch this." Sullivan sticks his fingers between his teeth and lets out a head-splitting whistle.

A rumble in the hall. The cups on the table begin to rattle. Frenzied pounding on the linoleum. *THUD!* Something the weight of a small truck skids into a wall in the rec room next door. The impact causes a framed picture to fly off its nail and crash onto the floor in a mess of glass shards. Victoria runs with the broom and dustpan to clean it up.

Careening around the corner, then galloping through the kitchen doorway toward us, is a slobbering, four-legged black beast. It reeks of dirty feet and tuna salad left too long in the sun. The creature halts three feet from the table and shakes, showering everyone with dirt and dander and sticky white spittle.

"What *is* that?" I whisper, turning around in my seat to get a better look.

Bad move.

The monster cocks its enormous head toward me. Its shiny black eyes glisten. Its gigantic tongue drips saliva like a broken faucet. Its entire body wags with something dangerously close to glee.

Then *WHOMP!*—my chair is upended. I'm on my back. Pinned to the floor. Slimed by the beast.

Screaming, I elbow my way out from under the hulking, stinking, hairy animal mass. I scramble to the sink as the beast emits a single ear-splitting *WOOF!* and bounds out the open kitchen door into the yard. Giggles fill the kitchen as I splash and spit and wipe and gargle.

When I finally turn to face the room, Dr. Fred wipes tears of laugher from his eyes. "That was Judy. She's half St. Bernard, half Newfie."

"And a few crumbs short of a Milkbone." Nicholas guffaws.

"She's only eighteen months old. Still a pup," Dr. Fred explains.

"And Sarah's new best friend," Taylor says.

"Better hers than mine," Johanna mumbles.

I shrug. "I'll survive."

I've survived a hell of a lot worse.

EIGHT

Ah, crap. For real.

Sunday morning, I get Poo Patrol.

You'd think that since all the dogs here eat the same brand of dog food, what comes out the back end would basically be the same too, right?

Ha.

Obviously small dogs create smaller poo mounds, and Judy, well…think Mount Everest. But it's the wide array of colors and textures and stenches that baffle me. Dr. Fred says that as long as I don't notice blood or worms or foreign objects in the stools, then all is well. Just shovel it all into the "poo pail" and dump—*"Dump, get it?"* Nicholas always says—the whole mess into the special composter out behind the barn. All in a day's community service, folks. Ask anyone here; it can be a shitty business.

Sunday afternoons, the Camp Dog Gone Fun "volunteers" have the option of being ferried over to the mainland for free time or having visitors ferried over to see us. Dr. Fred does the ferrying. I have no desire to go to the mainland, but when Dr. Fred comes back from his first run, my mother is with him.

"So how are you making out?" Mom asks as I drag two plastic lawn chairs into the shade of an old willow. Once we're seated, Mom passes me one of the two glasses of pink lemonade she's scored from the refreshment table Victoria set up on the porch beside the lodge.

She surveys the camp. The dogs have "relaxation time" on Sunday afternoons. Most are passed out in the shade beside the barn. A few of the younger and more sociable pooches are mingling with the visitors, vying for illicit snacks. Judy is locked in the "time out" kennel behind the lodge. (To make a long canine adventure story short, Judy'd been "mingling" too, until her exuberant leap onto Nicholas's grandmother's lap had collapsed the old woman's lawn chair, trapping Grams in the middle.)

"Making out? I haven't been making out with anyone," I reply, feigning indifference.

"Brownie would have liked it here," Mom adds, watching a sixteen-year-old sheltie and a three-legged beagle amble along the riverbank, sniffing for dead fish to roll in.

I have no wise-ass comeback to that. Truth is, I've thought about Brownie at least fifty times a day since arriving at Moose Island. And at least fifty times a day I've had to swallow my heart—and the bile that always accompanies those thoughts.

Brownie was my dog. A chocolate Lab. My father bought him for me when I was five. The same year I started school. In some families, dogs are pets; in my family, Brownie was a hostage. Don't tell, and the dog gets to live. And live he did, until just five months ago, when he died of cancer at the ripe old age of twelve.

"Don't you think Brownie would have liked it here?" Mom says, raising an eyebrow at my silence. "Christ, Sarah, it's not an algebra equation."

Trust me, it would be easier for me to answer if it *were* an algebra equation. "Yeah, Mom. Brownie'd have loved it here," I respond, taking a gulp of my lemonade and changing the subject quickly. Best to get Mom talking about shopping for books or some other stupid harmless topic. "Why were you in Ottawa yesterday?"

My mother hesitates. "Well…I have kind of a surprise. I was hoping to put off telling you now, but…"

Ah, hell. "What?" My heart sinks. I hate surprises. HATE THEM.

"I'm putting the restaurant on the market."

It's like Harold the concrete fighter pilot is flying at me all over again. "NO!!" I scream.

Heads—both human and canine—swivel in our direction from all over the island. A few of the dogs howl back at me. My mother shushes me and wrings her hands. "I knew you wouldn't like it, Sarah. But it's time. Past time.

It's been a year since your father died. Neither of us has any use for that space right now, and we need the money to pay your university fees next year. You know there wasn't much insurance money left after your father's bills were paid."

"You can't sell the restaurant!" I gasp. "Not yet!" The edges of the trees and the lodge are blurring, fading, falling into the river. I think I'm going to puke. Closing my eyes, I breathe deeply and will myself not to black out.

Through the fog, I hear Mom's voice, softer now, but with no less conviction. "I know you miss your dad, Sarah, but we have to let the restaurant go. The market is good right now."

"But—"

But what? What can I possibly say? Certainly not the truth. The ugly, ugly truth. That I'm sure the photos must be at the restaurant. All winter, I spent every evening that my mother was out, and every weekend she was with Tanner, scouring the house for the pictures. I hunted through the corners of the attic and the cellar, dredged the back of every closet, dug through each nook and cranny in the garage, looking for those Polaroids. I even got down on my hands and knees to check for loose floorboards after watching an episode of *CSI*.

Nothing.

"There'll be other restaurants, Sarah," my mother continues, "if you decide to follow in Dad's footsteps."

"What?"

"Don't you want to become a chef too? God only knows how much time Ian spent with you at that restaurant teaching you to cook. If you want, I can pick you up a few books at the library about grief and bring them out here next Sunday. Maybe I should have done that right after he died. It's just…you seemed to adjust so well at first."

My mother is brain-dead. How could she win—hands down—the local bookstore's *Harry Potter* trivia contest three years running and not know the first thing about her own daughter? Does she really think that my freak-out over selling the restaurant has something to do with me clinging to warm father-daughter memories? Does she really think I want the place for myself some day? Let's be clear: I want the place as much as I want an appendectomy without anesthetic. Probably less. Maybe if, just once, my mother had taken her damn nose out of the latest best-seller, she might have noticed what was really going on in my life. God, sometimes I hate her as much as I hated *him*.

I wish this was just another nightmare, but it's worse. It's real. "You won't find a buyer this summer, will you?" I choke out. Maybe there's some way to stall her.

My mother drains her lemonade and tips an ice cube into her hand. She rubs it across her forehead as if I'm giving her a headache.

"No, not likely," she sighs, as if that were a bad thing. "I really have to get in to clean first, take an inventory of the appliances, sort out details with the lawyers and the insurance people."

"Did Tanner talk you into this?"

Mom's eyebrows fly up to her hairline in surprise. Her eyeballs practically drop out of her head into her glass.

"That's crazy, Sarah. I haven't even mentioned my plans to Tanner yet. This doesn't concern him."

"It will if you marry him."

Now her face turns as red as her toenail polish. "You don't need to worry about *that* any time in the near future."

"Who said I was worried?" I fire back.

Bottom line, whether Tanner's involved or not, I have to find a way to get into my father's restaurant before my mother cleans and does inventory. I *must* find the pictures first. And when I find them, I'll burn them. Every last one of them. *And* the Hush Puppies shoe box I know they're stacked in. Dad probably thought he was a real class act, sticking with old-fashioned, expensive Polaroid photography even when digital became the norm, just so that I'd feel "assured" he wasn't sharing his prize pictures on the Internet. He always made sure I saw him put the developed photographs in the shoe box too, no doubt to "assure" me that he wasn't carrying them around in his pockets, where they might be discovered in the laundry by my mother, or pulled out by mistake while he hunted for pocket change to tip the paperboy. Unfortunately, my father's assurances never included letting me know *where* he hid the box between photo sessions. All my father's actions ever *did* assure me of was that going to all this trouble meant he was less likely to ever get caught and sent to jail.

Now I imagine myself spreading the ashes of the photos on my father's grave, taking care not to touch the poison ivy I planted there on Father's Day.

"Look Mom, why don't you wait until the fall?" I plead. "I can clean! I can do inventory!"

She frowns. "I don't think so, Sarah. I was hoping to—"

I lean forward in my chair. "But…you don't know what all the equipment and gadgets are called or what they're for."

Mom taps her nails on the side of her empty glass. "Well, you're right about that."

"And it's too big an undertaking for one person, isn't it?"

She sighs. "I'm sure Tanner will help. I just hate to put it off any longer."

And *I* hate to resort to whining and shameless begging, but what choice do I have?

"Please, Mom. Wait for me to come home before you go to the restaurant!" I grip the armrests of my chair so hard my knuckles crack. "Let me do it! Let me do the cleaning and inventory!" I pause and suck in air, try to work up a sniffle before I nail my point home. "It'll make me feel better about…letting go…"

I can't believe I just lied like that. Lying makes me itch. My arms and legs feel like they're covered in a million bug bites. If I were Pinocchio, my nose would be five feet long.

Mom's face softens like a pat of butter left out in the sun. With a sad smile, she reaches over and pats my hand. "I guess it can wait until September."

I relax back into the chair.

For about five seconds. Until I think about the first—and last—time I tried to "clean and do inventory" at my father's restaurant.

Yup, Dad's restaurant. Sarah's Place. That's where I "needed to get away" to the night I stole and crashed Tanner's car.

Better luck next time, I hope. Much better luck. Then my mother can sell—or torch—the damn place for all I care.

NINE

Every night, after the dogs have been fed, exercised and bedded down in the barn for the night, we "volunteers" are granted another dose of free time until lights-out at eleven.

"Have fun!" Dr. Fred exclaims, herding us into the musty lodge rec room. "Relax!" You'd think he was giving away all-expense-paid Hawaiian vacations.

But no.

"Just keep it legal," Victoria shouts from the kitchen. She plays bad cop to Dr. Fred's happy-go-lucky good cop; she's a firm subscriber to the don't-mess-with-me-and-everything-will-be-fine school of interpersonal relations. Victoria's quick to take to task anyone who puts one pinkie over her clearly set boundaries about swearing, cleaning up after the dogs (or oneself), surliness, rudeness and slacking off. Dr. Fred may drive the ship around camp, but Victoria keeps it afloat.

"I'm outta here," Brant exclaims, pumping a fist in the air. "Catch ya later, losers."

Each evening, Brant takes off in a dented aluminum motorboat for his parents' house over on the mainland. Brant lives so close to Moose Island that as long as he shows up for morning flagpole and stays until the end of evening chores, he can commute to and from home. He roars off in a cloud of gas fumes to play baseball and "cruise for chicks" in town (so he says), or (more likely, I think) play violent video games and research bomb-making techniques on the Internet in his basement bedroom. Nobody is sad to see him go.

Nicholas flips on the donated big-screen TV, his stomach rumbling like an approaching thunderstorm. Leaving the set on, he doubles back to the kitchen to beg Victoria for some corn kernels for the hot-air popper. Nicholas has been at Camp Dog Gone Fun for less than three weeks, but he's already lost twenty pounds. "It's pretty hard to gorge on Mars bars and Doritos on an island with no stores to shoplift from," he admits, his sad face drooping like a bullmastiff's. His grandmother hasn't been back to Moose Island with any super-sized care packages since the incident with Judy and the lawn chair. And unlike the rest of us "volunteers," who are sixteen or older, Nicky's court order stipulates that the thirteen-year-old can only leave the island on adult-supervised errands or, if necessary, for emergency medical treatment.

Bummer for him, but you can practically hear his heart and joints and intestines cheering.

Johanna leans against the oak-paneled wall as she does every evening, yap-yap-yapping into her cell phone—to her boyfriend, to her sister, to her friends, to her lawyer. She'll be at it for hours. Johanna gripes constantly, counting off on her long, French-manicured fingernails all the ways she hates island life. She's worked out a scheme to finish her community service hours giving homeless women manicures, but so far, the judge isn't buying. I think Johanna thought coming here would be easy, that she'd spend her days carrying little dogs around like accessories. She's so not prepared to deal with the four-legged misfits at Moose Island. Or their shit.

Taylor, as usual, is sprawled on the worn plaid couch, red and black felt pens in hand, gouging poetry into a beat-up spiral notebook. She openly shares her creativity with anyone who wanders by. "Hey, Nicky, come here. Listen to this." She beckons as Nicholas comes back into the rec room, a punch bowl full of air-popped popcorn and a pineapple juice box propped against his belly. "This one's called 'Uncle Joe's a Perv.'"

Taylor's poems make my skin crawl. I don't need to hear them to know she and I have shit in common. Maybe it is just the familiar stoop of Taylor's shoulders or the storm clouds in her eyes even on sunny days.

On the one hand, I envy her for being able to express her anger and pain. But on the other, I've always been suspicious of girls like Taylor—every school has a few—who play the victim card with so much enthusiasm. Is "sharing" really part of "healing," like one of Taylor's poems says, or does she just enjoy the attention and the sympathy and the shocked, uncomfortable looks her "Rhymes of Rebellion" generate around the rec room?

My goal is to destroy the images of my past, not display them. So I keep my distance.

Some nights, Sullivan digs deep into the Camp Dog Gone Fun "recreation cupboard," a battered metal filing cabinet full of his discarded childhood games and crusty art supplies. He cajoles Taylor, Nicholas and me into playing a game of Monopoly or Scrabble or Trivial Pursuit. Or he sets up a game of table hockey. Or he rolls out paper and starts a group mural, like he's some overzealous recreation therapist or something.

I'm pretty sure I wouldn't be as welcoming as Sullivan if a boatload of screwed-up kids were ferried into my life every summer, even if they were helping run the family kennel. But Sullivan bounces around the island, working as hard as everyone else and acting as if Camp Dog Gone Fun lives up to its name. He even takes his turn at daily meal prep, and he runs to the flagpole each morning to avoid Poo Patrol.

Tonight Sullivan materializes beside the balding corduroy recliner where I'm working on a crossword I've ripped out of a discarded newspaper.

He nudges me. Grins when I glance up. "Come up to my room for a sec?"

A rerun of *Law and Order* is on TV, but nobody's watching. Johanna is on the phone, having a fight with her boyfriend. Taylor is still slumped on the couch, scratch, scratch, scratching in her notebook. Nicholas sits beside her, seemingly unbothered by the elbow she jabs into his side with each exclamation point. He's already inhaled all the popcorn and juice and is chewing his fingernails like he'd starve without them.

I tuck my pen behind my ear and raise an eyebrow at Sullivan. "Why?"

"I just want to…talk to you about something," he says.

"Sullivan and Sarah, up in a tree," Nicholas sings from the couch. "*K-I-S-S-I…*"

"Fuck off, Nicky," I tell him.

"That's another five bucks for the cuss fund, Sarah!" Victoria yells from the kitchen.

"Put it on my tab," I mumble as I follow Sullivan up the stairs.

Call me a sucker for punishment.

Sullivan's summer bedroom is above the rec room, up a steep, narrow staircase. The room stinks of guy-sweat and rotten apple cores. There are worn Batman quilts on the bunk beds, a jumble of sports equipment piled up in a corner, books and magazines scattered around on the floor and the furniture, a pair of faded Fruit of the Looms crumpled near the door.

Clearly he hasn't brought me up here to impress me.

Sullivan swipes a stack of graphic novels off a chair and points for me to sit. "Are you any good at puzzles?" he asks, plunking himself down on his bottom bunk.

"What kind of puzzles? You mean crosswords?"

Sullivan rolls onto his stomach and thrusts an arm under the bed. He extracts a giant jigsaw box and holds it out for me to see, shaking it a little so that the two thousand pieces tumble around inside. The image on the box is a blurry head-and-shoulders photo of a German shepherd.

Frowning, I reach for the box to get a closer look and discover that the big photo of the German shepherd is made up of hundreds of smaller photos of all sorts of dogs. Light areas are created by images of Westies, Samoyeds, bull terriers and Old English sheepdogs. Black Labs, rotties, Dobermans and chows make up the shaded parts. Gold areas are golden retrievers, yellow Labs, shar-peis.

I know my dog breeds. When I was five years old and wanted a dog, I took a thick picturebook about dogs out of the library. I begged for a dog. I told my parents I needed one because I didn't have any brothers or sisters to play with. But really, I'd seen a show on Discovery Kids about police dogs and guard dogs and thought if I had a dog, it might protect me.

My father surprised me one day with a big, friendly chocolate Lab I named Brownie, who played with me but never protected me. I loved Brownie anyway, but never stopped wishing that he'd been some big, badass German shepherd with a taste for amateur photographers.

"So," Sullivan asks, jarring my attention back to the matter at hand. "Are you any good at this sort of thing?"

I pass the box back to him. "I guess."

Actually, I haven't done a jigsaw in years. I have fuzzy memories of a Little Mermaid puzzle box under the tree one Christmas when I was about eight or nine. I'd loved the Little Mermaid movies, watched them over and over. I loved all cartoons, because cartoon characters were just drawings. In seventh grade I'd been assigned an essay.

The topic was "What would you be if you could be anything?" I wrote about how I wished I could be a cartoon character so that I could erase myself. Not so that I'd disappear forever. Just so that I'd be invisible for a while. Until I grew up. Until the day I could move away and redraw myself any way I wanted. But even at age twelve, I knew that might be saying too much, that Mrs. Fallon might send me down to the counselor's office. So I ripped up that first essay and wrote some bullshit about wishing I could be an Arctic explorer. I hate the cold but liked the idea of wearing layers and layers of thermal underwear, snow pants and a heavy parka. Not an inch of skin showing.

"Is something wrong?" Sullivan asks, watching me wrap my arms around myself. It's hotter than hell in his room with the late evening sun streaming through the window, but I'm suddenly covered in goose bumps.

"No." But I can't stop imagining the image that would appear if my father's Polaroid collection was assembled into a big portrait of me. Fighting the useless urge to clench my eyes shut, I steer my head away from Sullivan, my gaze falling on my distorted reflection in the gray screen of the portable TV propped on his dresser. I see my straggly hair hanging around my head like a wrinkled brown hospital curtain. My oversized T-shirt. The baggy cargo shorts that swallow my hips. I look down at myself. Only my forearms and calves are tanned; the shorts and T-shirt are my only concession to the summer heat. Sometimes I envy Muslim women whose burkas cover everything but their eyes. Add a pair of mirrored sunglasses and I'd be good to go.

"Where did you get the puzzle?" I ask Sullivan. Not that I care, really. I just want him to shift his curious gaze from me back to the box.

"It's Dr. Fred's," he says, kicking off his canvas high-tops—bright orange today—and leaning back on the lower bunk, raising his skinny legs so that his feet push on the bottom of the top bed's springs. The enormous stuffed tiger that I know Sullivan won playing darts at Riverwood High School's Fall Fair topples off the upper bunk, landing belly up on the floor at my feet.

He shakes the puzzle box at me again. "Jigsaw Rover here was a gift a few years ago from some client who owns a hobby store. Dr. Fred cured his Dalmatian of an intestinal blockage. I have to put it together this summer. Dr. Fred wants to mount it on the wall of his mainland office."

"Why doesn't Dr. Fred do it himself?" I ask.

Sullivan shrugs. "He sucks at puzzles? He's too busy? He's too nearsighted to tell one piece from the other? He's been bugging me now for three summers to do it for him. I keep telling him no way, that it will take me forever. But now I've got no choice."

"Why's that?"

Sullivan laughs darkly. "It's punishment. Mom's grounded me until it's finished."

"Isn't having to live out here every summer punishment enough?"

Sullivan laughs. "Nah. I don't mind it. I like dogs. I like Dr. Fred. I like…"

"Hanging out with the juvies?" I offer.

"The volunteers, you mean," Sullivan says.

"Wouldn't you rather have a real summer job?"

Sullivan's neck glows pink. I realize what a stupid question that was. "Dr. Fred pays you for your work here, doesn't he?"

"Well...yeah."

And why wouldn't he? It's not like Sullivan has ever done anything really bad in his life.

Or maybe he has. Maybe he isn't Saint Sullivan after all.

"What did you do to get grounded?" I ask.

Sullivan sits up, swinging his legs off the bed and planting his gigantic feet on the belly of the tiger. His big hairy toes dig into the plush, making me wonder if someday Sullivan will grow into his feet the way big-breed puppies do.

"Remember yesterday? Mom sent me over to town in the boat to pick up the mail?"

Please. All I remember about yesterday were the hours and hours I'd spent washing and brushing and cutting the mats and burrs out of Judy's fur after she went rolling around in dog ecstasy through a big pile of brush compost. I hadn't even made it to the lodge for lunch. Take it from me: it might be easier to groom a temperamental gorilla than a St. Bernard-Newfie who keeps wiggling over onto her back for belly rubs and won't stop trying to wash your face with her tongue.

Sullivan continues. "Well...anyway...I didn't come back for five hours."

Is that really the worst thing Sullivan's ever done?

"See...I ran into some guys I knew from last summer. We went to the 7-Eleven for a while, got Slurpees, played some video games."

"Then what? You robbed the place?" I ask, joking. Sort of.

"Nooooo."

"So what's the big deal?"

Sullivan cracks his knuckles one at a time. "Well...the main dock was full when I got to town, so I tied the boat a ways down the shoreline. Near the park. Some joker must have come along, untied it and let it drift into the river. Remember how choppy the water was yesterday? The coast guard found the boat drifting out near the shipping lanes. They looked up the registration number and towed it back to Moose Island. Mom thought I'd drowned. I'm not a very strong swimmer."

"Don't you have a cell phone?" He has everything else, I think, peering around the messy room. Nice clothes, lots of sports equipment, books, a laptop, more colored high-tops than I've seen anywhere outside a shoe store. The Batman quilts need to go, but overall—

"I forgot to charge it last night," Sullivan says. "She couldn't reach me."

"Oops," I say, borrowing Johanna's favorite expression.

"Mom gave the coast guard my description. The coast guard gave the town cops my description. They spotted me walking back to the park to get the boat—of course I didn't even know it was gone—and told me that Victoria was freaking out."

"Wasn't she happy just to hear you were alive?"

Sullivan shrugged. "You'd think she would be, you know? But after she charged across to town in the boat to bring me home, she chewed me out the whole way back. About keeping my cell phone charged. About making sure I tie up the boat at a supervised dock. About losing track of time—"

"Lots of chewing. Bet you felt like a piece of rawhide," I interrupt, wondering if Sullivan has any inkling that his so-called problems are the stuff of a family sit-com. Or that my problems are—by comparison—the stuff of horror movies.

"So now the punishment," Sullivan explains. "I'm not allowed off-island until the puzzle is done. Mom believes in 'creative behavior management.'" He throws himself back on the bed. "Why can't she just smack me around the way some mothers do, then let it go? It would save us both time and—"

Maybe because she loves you more than that! I think. I jump up.

"Sarah…wait…"

"Cut to the chase, Sullivan," I say from the doorway. "You called me up here because you want me to help you with the puzzle, right? Why me?"

"Because Johanna would tell me to piss off if I asked her. Brant's not here in the evening; even if he were, he would tell me that jigsaws aren't cool. Taylor scares the hell out of me. Nicky might eat the pieces. Please…will you help me?"

"Is it still punishment if I help you?"

"That depends on you, I guess."

Ouch. Ten points for Sullivan.

Sullivan tosses the tiger aside, falls off the bed onto his knees and pleads with me. "Puh-leeeeeese, Sarah. Mom never said I had to do it alone. You know how she is, always preaching 'resourcefulness.' We can spread the puzzle out on this old ping-pong table that Dr. Fred keeps out in the storage shed. It's got a broken leg but we can find a way to prop it up."

"What's in it for me?"

Sullivan doesn't miss a beat. "Ratgut is in Ottawa the second week of August. I have two tickets. Won them last week on a radio call-in show. Ninth caller through. I've been *so* pumped about seeing them live. They're amazing. I thought about seeing if one of the guys I was hanging out with yesterday wanted to go with me—they all have cars— but if you help me *and* we get the puzzle done by then, I'll take you instead. How about it? We've got almost a month to finish the puzzle. If I ask, I'm sure my dad will come down from Riverwood to drive us there and back. It'll be a late night, but you're allowed off-island after evening chores, aren't you? Ratgut is…" Sullivan pauses, gets down on all fours, reaches down under his bed again and extracts a CD. He thrusts it up at me. "Here. Take this back to your cabin tonight. You have to listen all the way through to get a real feel for it. It's…*genius*."

Forget the stupid rock concert, I think, my brain spinning faster than any CD. Sullivan is my Golden Ticket.

My ticket into the city. My ticket into my father's restaurant without my mother knowing. My ticket to finding that hated shoe box full of old Polaroids. My ticket to freedom. My future.

My facial muscles relax for the first time since arriving at Camp Dog Gone Fun. I smile openly at another human being for the first time in what is probably years. "I'll do it." I reach out to shake Sullivan's hand, to seal the deal, hoping he doesn't take it too personally when I ditch him at the concert gates.

T E N

A week later, Sullivan bangs into the kitchen through the screen door. I'm slicing carrots for a beef stew.

"Nice job," he says, sidling up to me and watching as the thin slices fall onto the cutting board like orange dominoes. He grabs a few and inspects them. "How do you get them all the same thickness like this?"

"It's all in the wrist," I tell him, holding up my left arm and giving it a shake.

Now get out, Sullivan, I think. You smell like the dog barn. Your cheerfulness distracts me from my work.

And work it is.

Dr. Fred and Victoria have put me in charge of meals. All meals. It wasn't forced on me; they shamelessly spent this morning begging me to do it. Then, over lunch, the other "volunteers" and Sullivan voted unanimously to take on my dog duties, even Poo Patrol, if I'd take care of breakfast, lunch and dinner for the rest of the summer. It was the promise of no more Poo Patrol that clinched the deal.

("But not Judy. No way," Sullivan had said. "She's attached herself to you, Sarah, like a hairy overgrown leech. She's *your* Special Project.")

It was my spaghetti sauce last night that tipped everyone off to the fact that I could cook. *Really* cook. Maybe I should have stuck to thawing frozen lasagna or stirring up a mess of Hamburger Helper like everybody else does when they draw the Meal Prep straw at flagpole. Maybe I should have known that adding those extra veggies and spices to the Prego last night was a bad idea.

Cooking is…well…it disgusts me a bit that I've somehow absorbed my father's talent for slicing and dicing and sautéing and whipping. It kind of creeps me out that I can stir a pound of ground beef, an onion, some mushrooms, two cans of stewed tomatoes, a mess of dried herbs and a big pot of noodles into something that even Johanna, Camp Dog Gone Fun's wannabe anorexic, can't help but shovel in by the forkful. But part of me likes being good at something, so I'm secretly pleased when they ask me to cook.

And I can't believe that I'm already thinking ahead to tomorrow. I'm planning to set my alarm a half hour early to stir up some whole-wheat waffle batter and chop red peppers for an omelet. Next I'll be wondering if that sunny dirt pile behind the lodge would support a small tomato patch.

"Did you know," Sullivan continues, popping carrot slices into his mouth and talking with his mouth open, "that when Michelangelo painted the ceiling of the Sistine

Chapel, he portrayed Adam receiving life from God through his left hand?"

"Did you know, Sullivan," I reply, "that while only ten percent of the general population is left-handed, fifteen to thirty percent of mental patients are left-handed?"

That should give him something to think about. Somewhere else, hopefully.

"Julia Roberts is left-handed," Sullivan states, undeterred.

"Here. Taste this." I shove a wooden spoon dripping with stew into Sullivan's mouth.

He smacks his lips. "Incredible. Listen, can I come with you later? When you go out in the canoe? With Judy?"

As part of Judy's "program," I paddle around the island each evening in an old beat-up aluminum canoe while Judy swims beside me. We never travel too far from the island. I tell myself that it's because a) I'm no hotshot at water sports (I lied to Victoria about being able to swim) and b) if Judy tires, she can quickly make it to shore for a rest. Except that a) I got the hang of canoeing early on (making tipping, and therefore swimming, avoidable) and b) it seems Judy never tires. On land, she's a clumsy, lumbering, knuckle-headed oaf; in the water, she's a mermaid with energy to burn and a thick layer of body fat to keep her afloat. (Whatever the shortcomings of her previous owners, Judy appears to have been well fed.) The *real* reason I stick to shore is because on warm summer evenings, the tourists are out on the St. Lawrence in droves. The river is a regatta. Some of the smaller boats come dangerously close to Moose Island—not that I give a rat's ass if they scratch their boats on the rocks, but the tourists have cameras and they'll point them at anything, even at me and Judy. I just know that *Enormous Dog Swimming Beside Girl in Canoe* is begging to be photographed and published on the cover of some Thousand Islands travel brochure.

"Aren't you grounded?"

Sullivan chews thoughtfully on another piece of carrot. "Mom said it was okay to go out in the canoe with you. As long as we don't venture over to town."

"What if we 'ventured over' to upstate New York instead?" I joke, waving my knife toward the south-facing window.

"Or not. Anyway, I just thought…the water's a bit rough out there tonight. You might want some…help?"

"It's not *that* rough." First the puzzle, now this. Sullivan is getting clingier than Judy. If I were one of those popular girls from the chick-lit novels I read in the school library, I might think that Sullivan was flirting with me.

What the hell am I thinking? It can't be that.

"Well?" Sullivan persists.

I can see out the window that the wind has picked up a little. And wake from some of the powerboats can be daunting.

"I guess an extra set of puny triceps can't be a bad thing."

ELEVEN

After dinner, we head down to the dock. It's Sullivan's canoe, so I let him take the stern. I hate it, though. I can feel his eyes watching me, boring into the back of my skull like a couple of corkscrews.

"So…that dog puzzle's really coming along," he says.

I'm not sure if he's asking for confirmation or just stating the obvious, so I stay quiet.

"I'd say we placed at least one, maybe two hundred pieces last night? Not bad, since we only worked at it for a couple of hours. It's hard, that puzzle."

"Not so hard," I tell him.

And it'd be way easier if Sullivan spent more puzzle time puzzling instead of yapping.

"Think we'll get it all done by the concert?" he asks. "It's only four weeks away."

"We damn well better," I mumble.

"I can't hear you!" Sullivan calls up.

"Yes!" I shout. "We'll get it done!"

Sullivan splashes my back with his next stroke. "Admit it, Sarah, you loved that CD I lent you."

I need to maintain my cover, but here's the truth: the CD sucks. Ratgut is just a bunch of screaming losers. Their "instrumentals" sound like ice cubes in a blender.

But I swivel in my seat to face Sullivan. "Ratgut is *amazing*! Just like you said, Sullivan. *Genius*! I can't *wait* to get to that concert!"

Well, at least that last part is true.

Sullivan is encouraged by my enthusiasm. "Listen, maybe we could...you know...rush through evening chores that day? Get an early start to the city? Make time to stop somewhere for pizza before the concert?"

Sullivan's not trying to turn this little concert outing into a date, is he?

Nah. I lay my paddle across the gunwales and take a deep breath. Besides, once I ditch him at the concert, Sullivan will know that I'm just using him. That I am not someone he should pursue even a basic, no-frills friendship with.

He deserves better than me.

Sullivan doesn't wait for an answer. "I called my dad today. He remembers you from school and agreed to come down to Gananoque that night and hang out with a guy he knows from his teachers' college days. He'll let me drive his car to the city and back."

"And Victoria is okay with you going with me?"

"Sure, as long as I get the puzzle done first. That's our deal. She'll run us over to the mainland to hook up with Dad.

Then, as long as I call her every hour on the hour to let her know I'm still alive, we're cool."

"I mean…she's okay with you going with *me*?" I ask. "One of the…"

"'Volunteers'? Sure. She likes you, Sarah," Sullivan says; then he laughs. "Your cuss fines are single-handedly funding this summer's supply of rawhide and tennis balls."

"Very fucking funny. So why is she so overprotective?"

Chewing his lip, Sullivan points over my shoulder with his paddle. "Hey, watch out for that driftwood!"

I swivel back around to face front.

No driftwood.

"I don't see—"

"So…how about that pizza before the concert?" Sullivan persists.

Judy is leading the canoe by a good thirty feet. I speed up my stroke to close the gap, wondering about Sullivan's sudden evasiveness, relieved that he's not really the wide-open, brightly colored picturebook he always seems to be.

"Sarah?"

"Yeah?"

"Pizza?"

"Uh…sure. Sounds…great."

What choice do I have, anyway? I have to do whatever it takes to get into my father's restaurant this summer without my mother knowing. I should be glad that all Sullivan wants is help with his puzzle—and now pizza.

Except I am wrong. Sooo wrong. Because after canoeing around the island and putting away our paddles and life vests, Sullivan blindsides me.

He kisses me. Right there in the damp, musty-smelling darkness of the boathouse.

I am NOT cut out for teen romance. Kissing happens to other girls. Girls in novels with glossy pink covers. Girls with pretty clothes and bright smiles.

So why the hell am I kissing him back? Why is my heart pounding with excitement, not fear? Why does his mouth taste like warm cinnamon buns, not disgust?

T W E L V E

It doesn't take much time for life to get back to normal. Meaning crappy.

Fifteen minutes later I've disentangled my tongue from Sullivan's, towel-dried Judy and settled her down in the barn. I am walking, a bit dazed, my lips still tingling, toward my cabin to change out of my splash-damp clothes before returning to the kitchen to slice up some banana bread for evening snack.

Brant yells up to me from the dock. He's sitting in his crappy tin can of a motorboat, about to leave for home. "Hey! Sarah-ha-ha! Get my cell phone? It's on my bunk."

I hate—*hate*—him calling me Sarah-ha-ha. And I know that "please" would be too much to expect from Brant. But I mumble, "Yeah, sure," since I'm going that way anyway.

Like everyone else here, Brant gets his own small cabin. Old Mr. Moose had originally built the five tiny sheds to house his summer guests and housekeeping staff. But unlike the other Camp Dog Gone Fun "volunteers,"

Brant only uses his private quarters to change clothes, blast music, lift weights between dog duties and—I suspect—pop steroids and admire his muscles in his tiny bathroom mirror.

I push open his cabin door (there are no locks at Camp DGF. Something to do with fostering trust, blah, blah, blah) and gasp at the mess. I'm no neat freak, but the crumpled chip bags, moldy crusts, Coke cans erupting with ants, wet towels, heaps of sour-smelling workout clothes...it's truly revolting.

It's only after I rifle through a pile of dog-eared *Sports Illustrated* magazines and cheesy-smelling socks on Brant's cot that I locate his cell phone, wedged under a crumpled beach towel thrown across his bare foam mattress. Brant's phone isn't the no-frills kind I have and rarely use (the only person who ever calls is my mother). His is an expensive model, one that texts, takes photos, records videos, plays Mp3s and would probably make you a grilled cheese sandwich if you asked it to.

Phone in hand, I turn to hightail it back out into the evening breeze, and my peripheral vision catches sight of an open magazine poking out from under Brant's cot. I nudge the magazine a few inches farther with my toe and gape down at the naked woman with fake boobs and fake hair and a fake smile sprawled on a white wicker beach chair.

I know that magazines like this one exist. And that guys like Brant read them—though "reading" is absolutely the wrong verb. And I know that if a grown woman wants to take her clothes off for money, or the sick thrill of having guys like Brant jerk off to her naked image, it's not illegal.

But that doesn't stop me from clamping my hand over my mouth to avoid adding a layer of post-dinner puke to Brant's already filthy floor.

Shaky-legged and gulping oxygen, I finally make it back to the dock and toss Brant his phone.

"Took you long enough," he says, catching it in one hand. He revs his boat's engine and takes off across the river before I can gather enough breath to tell him to go to hell.

My father might like the company.

THIRTEEN

At breakfast a few days later, Dr. Fred drops two books into my lap: *Loving Your Large-Breed Puppy* and *Dog Training for Dummies.*

I peer up from my blueberry pancakes. "Is this some kind of a joke?"

Dr. Fred's eyes sparkle with benevolence. "Thought they might help. With Judy."

Oh, come on. No one will ever write a book to help Judy. Think about it; even the title would be overwhelming. *That Crazy Bitch: Coping with the Oversize, Overactive, Overaffectionate and Underachieving She-pup from Hell.*

But Dr. Fred looks so enthusiastic and...hopeful.

"Okay," I say. "Thanks."

Before it's time to start slicing and dicing veggies for the lunch salad, I take Judy down to the beach for her morning aerobics. A solid hour of stick fetching in the river is the only activity that exhausts her. It frees me up to cook lunch while she curls up under the kitchen table like a hibernating black bear.

Judy and I have developed a stick-throwing routine: As soon as we get to the beach, Judy bounds off along the shore to find a stick of appropriate width and length. Then she drops it at my feet. I pick it up, take random aim and whip it as far as I can out into the St. Lawrence. I don't worry much about the current; it's not all that strong this close to the mainland, plus I'm pretty sure Judy could swim up Niagara Falls if she ever got the opportunity.

Judy dashes out into the river after the stick, like a lifeguard after a drowning victim. She fetches the stick, bounds back out of the water, drops it at my feet and shakes, spraying water and sand and green river slime all over me.

If I'm not quick enough to begin the routine again, Judy nudges me into action. Nudges me the way a speeding snowplow would "nudge" Frosty. Resistance is futile.

Today, during the short periods when Judy is out in the water retrieving, I plunk down on one of the granite boulders littering the shoreline and flip through Dr. Fred's books. Who knows, maybe I'll learn something. I just hope that Dr. Fred won't mind a few water-warped, sand-gritty pages when I return them.

The basic premise of both books, I find out right away, is that to deal with the "difficult" dog, the human has to accept that he or she is not the dog's playmate. So when it comes to Judy, I must promote myself to head honcho.

Alpha dog. *I* have to be the one to initiate the stick game, not Judy. *I* have to enter or exit the kitchen ahead of Judy—not hold the door open for her, letting her charge in first. *I* have to exercise leadership and take more responsibility for Judy's behavior.

The theory makes sense, but I don't know if I'm up for it. My whole life I've been told what to do. Turn to page sixteen, do problems six through eleven, the school told me. So I did. Take off those panties or the dog dies, my father told me. So I did. After my father died, I wondered if it was safe to start standing up for myself. Taking the initiative. Say cheese, Tanner told me. I told him to piss off, and then I stole his car.

What did my efforts get me? Community service.

But like it or lump it, Judy's success or failure this summer rests with me. And seriously, how hard can it really be to teach Judy to follow some basic commands like *Sit*, *Down* and *Stay*? If Rocky, the eight-week-old blind Pomeranian, can learn to do it, and if Henry, the fifteen-year-old three-legged German shepherd, can do it, and if Delia, the deaf, sock-eating Dalmatian, can do it, why can't Judy do it?

Judy brings her stick to me again, drops it at my feet and nudges me so hard that I tumble sideways off the boulder. She gallops back over to the shoreline in anticipation of my next toss and barks four times.

Judy telling me what to do. As usual.

"Forget it, Judy," I mumble, picking myself up off the beach and brushing dirt and pebbles off my arms and legs. "Today *I'm* in charge."

Ignoring the stick at my feet, I set the books on the boulder and take ten steps backward, away from Judy.

"Judy, come," I say.

Judy just stands at the water's edge, tongue lolling, entire rear end wagging, waiting for the stick.

"Judy! Come!" I command, more firmly this time.

Judy cocks her head. Her bushy right eyebrow shoots up questioningly.

"JUDY! COME!"

A group of gulls lands on a boulder a hundred feet down the shore. Judy forgets all about the stick and me and charges off after the big white birds, barking as if a UFO has just landed on the beach.

"You stupid mutt," I grumble, watching Judy pick up speed as the gulls, screeching, take off over the river. Shaking my head in disgust—at Judy or my own incompetence, I'm not sure which—I plunk back down on the boulder and keep reading.

Use treats to reward positive behavior, the book says.

That I can manage.

"Judy!" I bellow down the beach after her. "COOKIE!"

Aha! Judy stops in her tracks and whips her head toward me. At least the stupid mutt isn't deaf. I feel a surge of success. But then Judy notices that all I'm holding up is a mini-Milkbone, just like all the mini-Milkbones I've been feeding her all morning, one for each time she sticks her soggy nose into my shorts pocket. She turns her attention back to the birds.

I slam the book shut and let my shoulders sag in defeat.

I've failed at dog training, or Judy training in any case. "It's not rocket science, for shit's sake!" I can imagine my mother chastising me. And she'd be right, because I remember, back when I was six or seven, getting Brownie to sit for Cheerios, carrot slices, little bone-shaped kibbles—he wasn't picky. But Brownie was a smart dog. A calm dog. A good dog.

Not a maniac like Judy.

I know that Dr. Fred expects more of me. I know that if I go to him and tell him I can't do it, he'll just grin and give me a pep talk about not giving up on Judy—and myself—so soon.

And it's not like I have the actual option of throwing in the towel anyway. I'm stuck at Camp Dog Gone Fun for the rest of the summer. Judy is my punishment, my community service. My work here isn't necessarily supposed to be easy—or fun. That's what Victoria would say. So I guess I'll just have to up the ante with Judy, start from scratch.

Wait a minute. *From scratch.*

A lightbulb—an *oven* light—pops on in my head.

FOURTEEN

I wedge the last of the crusty lunch dishes into the rattly dishwasher, slam the door shut and push the ON button. I've tied Judy to the shady side porch and tossed her a rawhide loop to chew on. It's the size of a mountain-bike tire; it should keep her busy for at least an hour.

Time to get to work. Hi-ho, hi-ho, as Nicholas goes around camp singing.

Into a big mixing bowl, I scoop a few cups of whole-wheat flour, a cup of cornmeal and a big bowl of leftover oatmeal from breakfast. I crack three eggs into the mix, pour in a monster can of mixed vegetables and add just enough salt-free chicken broth to make a nice pliable dough.

Victoria rushes past me on her way outside for her midafternoon jog. She's got a trail worn around the perimeter of the island. Victoria does fifteen laps of this trail every single day—heat wave, downpour, impending hurricane, nothing stops her. Sullivan told me that during the winter months, when his mother and Dr. Fred live on the mainland, Victoria runs along Highway 2 every morning, dodging the transport trucks and potholes and roadkill. I'm sure some people would call it dedication and stamina. Probably the same people who gave Victoria all those framed *Counselor of the Year* awards she's hung around the lodge as a reminder that she's "here for us."

"Do we have any cookie cutters?" I ask.

Victoria stops in her tracks, jogs across the kitchen and pulls open a cupboard full of all sorts of dusty kitchen junk. She rummages around a bit, finally extracting two cookie cutters: a Christmas tree and a snowflake. "'Tis not exactly the season," she says, handing them to me anyway.

"They'll do," I reply, switching the oven on to preheat and pulling out several cookie sheets from the drawer underneath.

"Those aren't chocolate chips," Victoria says, sidling up to me and peering over my shoulder at the dough. "They're *green*. Is that a—"

"It's a pea." Now run off, would you? Next to being ogled myself, I hate having what I'm doing ogled.

Victoria's nose wrinkles. "Mmm…interesting. Does this recipe have a name?"

"Mmm…Judy's…Doggie Delights?"

"Gotcha," she laughs, and with a spin, a wave and a swoosh of her red ponytail, Victoria's out the door. (The rest of us humans may have descended from primates, but Victoria and Sullivan descended from Tasmanian devils.)

An hour later, forty-eight trees and fifty-six snowflakes are cooling on the counter. They are crispy but not burned; crunchy, just the way Dr. Fred says a good dog treat should be. He's totally into plaque busting.

Brant saunters in on break from his dog chores, grabs a bottle of water from the fridge and—

"Brant! Don't!"

Too late. He pops a snowflake into his mouth.

"Bleckkkkk! Ewwww! Ickkkkk!" A horror movie plays out across his face.

I laugh. I've been doing that more and more lately— laughing. I feel so surprised when it happens, embarrassed almost, like I've let out a loud unexpected fart.

"Sarah-ha-ha, you forgot to add the sugar," Brant tells me.

"No, I didn't."

Sucker for punishment, he bites into another cookie, a Christmas tree this time. He pulls the remainder of the cookie away from his mouth and squints at it. "Is that...a carrot? And what's this other chunk? *A green bean?* You made *vegetable* cookies?"

"I didn't make them for you."

"Did I hear someone say...cookies?" Nicholas hurries through the kitchen door, wiping dirty ribbons of sweat from his face with the hem of his T-shirt. Sniffing the air like a hungry bear, he reaches over my shoulder and snatches a Christmas tree from the tray. He takes a bite. "Mmmph...not bad, Sarah. But...well..." He sucks crumbs off his top teeth. "Not very good either." But he swallows the cookie anyway and stuffs three more in his pocket for later.

Brant tosses what's left of his snowflake out the screen door to Judy. From the kitchen window, I watch Judy drop the rawhide, sniff the cookie tentatively, then suck it up like a turbocharged Shop-Vac.

Amen.

Nicholas and Brant leave to get back to their dog duties, muttering as they stomp down the porch stairs about how they hope I get back to making banana bread and apple crisp soon.

When they've wandered back to the dog barn, I prop open the kitchen door and step out of the heat of the kitchen onto the shady porch. I close my eyes and turn my face up into the stiff river breeze that blew this morning's smog downriver. Fresh air flows through my hair and down my neck. It may be the only moment of quiet, and the closest thing to a shower, I'll have time for today.

My break has lasted all of fifteen seconds when a cold nose nudges my hand. I open my eyes and peer down at Judy. Stringy beige remains of the rawhide chew are stuck to her neck and front paws. Snowflake cookie crumbs are stuck to her nose. I untie her from the porch railing. "I knew you'd like my cookies," I tell her, giving her ears a good scratch.

Judy barks and shoves past me into the kitchen where she knows by smell that there are more snowflakes. Risking being trampled to death, I lunge in front of Judy and grab a snowflake cookie off the tray before she can jump up onto the counter to help herself.

"Judy! Sit!" I yell, trying to sound like what the books call "enthusiastic and authoritative."

Judy sits. The sound of her big butt plunking onto the kitchen tile is like…music. (Percussion, but music nevertheless.)

I give Judy the cookie. She gobbles it up and immediately tries to leap up on the counter for another.

I block her again, bracing myself for the thud and subsequent bruising as Judy hip-checks me into the counter. "Judy, sit," I command.

Judy sits.

I give her a cookie.

Judy sits again. This time without a command.

I give her another cookie and throw my arms around her hairy bulk. Over Judy's smelly shoulder—what the hell has the rotten mutt been rolling in now?—I see Dr. Fred standing in the kitchen doorway, grinning from ear to ear. He applauds as if Judy and I are rock stars.

"Victoria ran into me—literally," he explains. "She told me you were baking," he adds, giving me a thumbs-up. "Good work."

Hot with embarrassment, I mumble thanks and turn my back on Judy just long enough to put a half-used carton of eggs back in the fridge.

Bad move.

In the five seconds it takes for me to shove the carton in and slam the fridge door, Judy has lunged up on the counter and scarfed down at least another dozen cookies from the tray on the counter. Dr. Fred just stands there busting a gut laughing. In response, Judy gives Dr. Fred and me a "joke's on you" flick of her tail as she bounds out the unlatched screen door, down the porch stairs and onto the field, her back end dancing across the island in cookie-induced euphoria.

Okay, so Judy's not a one-session wonder dog. But at least I know she isn't stupid either. Judy has issues, but she also has…potential.

It's food for thought.

FIFTEEN

Late the next afternoon I am back in the kitchen, this time making dinner. Chicken fajitas with homemade salsa.

Down the hall in his office, Dr. Fred is whistling "How Much Is That Doggie in the Window" as he tabulates the week's food receipts.

He and Nicholas have just returned from the weekly grocery run. I sent them over to town two hours ago with a three-page shopping list. (A list pared down, I might add, from my original nine-page "wish list." Victoria told me that I needed to keep my menus within the Camp Dog Gone Fun food budget and the limited selection at the local No Frills. I'm not sure how many ground beef and macaroni miracles I can perform in one summer, but I'll give it a shot.)

Nicholas is in the kitchen too, tossing bags of apples and pears into the crisper and glowing with pride. Dr. Fred, the optimist, believes it's because Nicky resisted shoplifting during his so-called adult-supervised outing.

Ha.

"Look what I stole," Nicholas whispers to me. He reaches a hand down the back of his baggy jeans and extracts roughly fifteen packs of Trident gum from the waistband of his underwear. "Maybe I can keep off the weight I've lost here at camp." (Nicholas always says "at camp," like Camp Dog Gone Fun is a flipping Boy Scouts retreat or something and he'll go back to his grandmother at the end of the summer with a Dog Grooming badge or a carved wooden key chain in the shape of a bone.) "Brant said if I start lifting weights too, that I'll really be able to *wow the hot babes* when I start high school this fall."

Brant's advice isn't worth two steaming Chihuahua turds. "You won't wow *any* babes if you end up in jail," I tell him.

Taylor traipses into the kitchen and reaches over Nicky's head for a bottle of water. "Not unless your idea of a hot babe is a hairy, tattooed, drug-addicted ax murderer named Bubba," she says, chugging down her water quickly and wiping her chin with her wrist.

"They don't put you in jail for stealing gum," Nicky sneers.

"They will if you keep getting caught," Taylor tells him.

"Or if you start filling your Fruit of the Looms with iPods and jewelry," I add.

Nicholas reaches into the crisper and pelts a red grape at my head. "Well, Miss Mario Andretti, at least I never stole a car!"

"Fuck off, Nicky," I say, but I can't help laughing and whipping the grape back at him. He ducks, catching it in his mouth.

"Ten points for Captain Underpants!" he shouts. "Hey, Sarah, did you know that if you write your name backwards, it spells *harass*?"

"You won any spelling bees lately, Nicky?" Taylor laughs, chucking her water bottle into the recycling bin and heading back outside.

"You want a stick?" Nicholas asks me, holding out two open packs of gum. "You like spearmint or cinnamon?"

I take one of each. What the hey.

Nicholas finally goes to hide his stash in his cabin, and I enjoy about thirty seconds filled only with the sizzle of chicken strips browning in a pan before Sullivan crashes through the kitchen door, his big feet bare. I glance out the kitchen window and spot his red-and-green-plaid high-tops strewn on the field. "Stepped in dog you-know-what. Be back in a flash." He makes a beeline through the kitchen to the rec room and then pounds upstairs to his room.

He's back in less than a minute, wearing enormous black flip-flops that look like scuba flippers. He leans against the dishwasher, watching me chop onions and mushrooms and peppers.

"Don't slice off your fingers," he warns. "It's a fact that lefties like you, Sarah, are fifty-four percent more likely than right-handers to have accidents with tools."

"Where do you come up with this stuff?" I ask.

"Oprah did a show on left-handedness one day when I was off sick from school. She's a leftie too."

"So was Jack the Ripper," I say, giving the chicken strips a toss in the pan.

"You look like Martha Stewart," Sullivan remarks.

I reach around Sullivan for the garlic press. "Martha got sent to *real* jail."

Sullivan's ears turn the color of the red peppers on the cutting board. "No, no. That's not what I meant. You look like...who's that other woman...the one with the funny accent...she used to be on TV too...Julia Child?"

"She's dead."

"Sorry, I mean—"

"And she was *old*. And *fat*."

"I just *mean*...you look like a real chef."

"Genetic mutation," I say, cringing at the compliment. Not everyone in Riverwood knew my father, *the* Ian Greene of Sarah's Bistro, but still, his "unfortunate" demise was written up in all the regional newspapers. Local tragedy, blah, blah, blah.

Sullivan smacks the side of his head. "Right. Your dad owned that restaurant up in the city. By the way, sorry about what happened...you know...to him."

"Don't be," I say, blinking hard. I mean it—and then some. But the damn onions are making my eyes water. I sure hope that Sullivan doesn't think I'm crying over my father.

Like *that* would ever happen.

Here's something you should know: if my father hadn't given me one huge, skin-crawling reason to hate his guts for all eternity, there were a million small reasons why I loved him.

Take away his despicable Polaroid camera, and I had a dad who helped with homework, showed up at all my school concerts, and patiently taught me how to separate eggs, use his fancy food processor and melt chocolate in the double boiler. He took me to petting zoos, museums and parks on weekends. He encouraged me to name my dog after my favorite dessert.

Dad knew how to make Mom laugh, how to make her agree to some outlandish kitchen purchase, how to make her day with flowers, *even* how to get her nose out of the latest best-seller for a night out. In a town where divorced or battling parents were the norm, I never had to deal with screaming or slamming doors or weeklong parental silences.

Like Sullivan, my father made a big deal of my left-handedness. He read up about right-brain dominance and told me that left-handed people were supposed to be super creative. He signed me up for music lessons: piano, then violin, then clarinet. I sucked at all of them. Same with painting classes and the pottery workshop. Ditto for ballet and jazz dance. Even my efforts at a summer creative-writing camp were to great literature what nails are to the blackboard—or so the instructor said.

But I aced cooking. And while my father can take the credit for teaching me the basics, it was me who, that summer between sixth and seventh grade, went a bit crazy with it. I experimented with everything from the spices in Dad's old family chili recipe to the consistency of the hot fudge he poured over his hand-churned ice cream.

Don't misunderstand me. It's not that I like cooking so much. I just like being good at something. Recipes came—still come—naturally to me, in much the same way that I think piano concertos must come to Jake Malone, the autistic boy who lives down the street from Mom and me in Riverwood. So I rolled with it.

"Earth to Sarah…"

Sullivan reaches over my shoulder and grabs a slice of red pepper. He bites into it, chews thoughtfully and swallows. "How do you like it here?" he asks me.

I bet Sullivan asks himself that same question a few times a day, especially since he's been grounded. More than once I've overheard him humming the theme song to *Gilligan's Island*.

I set my knife down beside the sink. "Well, Sullivan, I'd say that most days the whole Camp Dog Gone Fun experience rates somewhere between a Disney World vacation and going to the dentist."

Sullivan pops another slice of pepper into his mouth. As I watch him chew, he reaches out and tucks a strand of my hair—an escapee from my only-when-I-cook ponytail—behind my left ear. He takes the rare opportunity to study my face. "More puzzle work tonight, right?" he asks.

I want to turn away. I can feel my face burning, the skin on my cheeks crawling. But Sullivan's blue-eyed gaze has my head in a vise grip.

If he's going to kiss me again, I wish he'd just do it. Maybe I even want him to.

Victoria makes Sullivan eat a lot of veggies, so his breath is always fresh, like a salad. And I like the way his skinny hands rested so firmly on my shoulders during that quick first kiss in the boathouse, like he knew that if he didn't keep me grounded, I'd fly out of there like a startled seagull. Truth is, I felt safe in the darkness with him.

But I can't stand having Sullivan stare at me like this under the hot kitchen lights.

Because I'm sure that the truth, the ugly truth, is written in bold letters somewhere on my face.

So I step back and grab a serving spoon off the counter. Wielding it like a sword, I back Sullivan out the kitchen door.

Sullivan checks his watch. "Later, 'Gator," he calls over his shoulder as he bounds out the screen door and takes a flying leap from the top of the porch stairs to the ground. It's his job today to round up the seven old dogs with hypothyroidism, the four old dogs with diabetes and the five young dogs with epilepsy for their twice-daily trek into Dr. Fred's office for their medications.

I reach up to switch the range fan on HIGH.

SIXTEEN

Sometimes, in the evenings, after the dogs are all bedded down in the barn and Brant's left for home, Dr. Fred lights a bonfire down on the small strip of sandy gravel on the south shore that he calls the beach and invites the rest of us to join him. Sometimes he gives us geography and history lectures to fill the time. Sometimes he does chemistry experiments or imparts wilderness survival tips. Mostly he tells stories; gruesome Chinese fairy tales and synopses of old Hollywood horror movies are his favorites. It seems that Dr. Happy-All-the-Time has an edge after all. I like it.

Sometimes Nicholas brings down his guitar. When she found out he played a little, Victoria paid to have it couriered from his grandmother's house.

"Keeping your hands busy with constructive things is never bad, Nicholas," she told him the morning she brought it over to the island from town.

Brant the sicko piped up. "I know how to keep *my* hands busy." He made a jerk-off motion behind her back.

Anyway, back to Nicky, pudgy fingers and all. He's not a bad guitar player. No Carlos Santana, but not terrible either.

But then there's Johanna, shrieking out old Celine Dion ballads. Johanna is convinced—*hello, delusional*—that she'll be a huge star someday. On the bright side, Johanna's singing keeps the biting insects away. And the dogs love it; they howl in the barn like crazed backup singers.

When all else fails, Taylor is always eager to offer up some of her tortured poetry for critique.

Me? I put together ingredients for S'mores. Good enough.

Tonight Dr. Fred begins his campfire session with a lecture on the history of the Thousand Islands region.

I can't believe that the big heap of granite rubble they call Camp Dog Gone Fun is actually a remnant mountain peak—one of more than a thousand remnant peaks poking out of the St. Lawrence River. Join all the peaks together and they make up an ancient mountain chain that was scoured, molded and eventually flooded by several glacial advances and melts.

I stare into the bonfire's flames, unsettled by the knowledge that the Thousand Islands were once interconnected. Does it mean that each individual—even me—might actually be part of a bigger "we"? That maybe humanity is just a different type of mountain chain?

Some people might feel all warm and fuzzy about that possibility. Me? I feel crowded.

Sullivan isn't around tonight. Grounded or not, it's Thursday, which means he's back in Riverwood, having his legislated weekly visit with his dad. During the school year, when Sullivan lives with his father, he visits Victoria and Dr. Fred every Saturday. Sounds like a complicated pain-in-the-ass arrangement to me, but Sullivan says it's the only life he's known since he was three years old. He doesn't even remember his parents ever living together. He says both of them blame their divorce on Rusty, an Irish setter they owned when Sullivan was a baby. Rusty developed a seizure disorder. During a particularly rough patch, Victoria started spending more time with Dr. Fred than with Sullivan's dad.

Oops, as Johanna would say.

After the divorce, Mr. Vickerson got custody of Sullivan. Victoria got custody of Rusty. Dr. Fred doesn't seem the type to break up a marriage. Then again, no one would have guessed that my father was a perv either. Who would have thought he'd have had the time, between operating a successful restaurant, taking part in local fundraisers, running six miles a day and being seen around town playing the role of good husband and father?

Moral of *this* story: Adults can't be trusted. Maybe *no one* can be trusted. Maybe you can't even trust yourself.

Nice world.

I'm not sorry that Sullivan is away for the night. I need a break. We've been spending every spare dog-free, food-free moment in Dr. Fred's storage shed under a hot bare bulb, working that German shepherd jigsaw puzzle on top of a three-legged ping-pong table propped up with milk crates. The puzzle is big, the pieces are small, the lighting is harsh and Sullivan keeps kissing me, so it's taken hours and hours of no-longer-free time for Sullivan and me to get the jigsaw just one-quarter done. And with over three weeks still to go before the concert, my biggest worry is keeping the shed door barricaded 24/7. It takes no imagination to picture Judy storming the place, tipping over the table and destroying our hard work.

I know I could/should be in the shed alone now, working on the puzzle, going at it great guns without the distraction of Sullivan's fast-flowing river of conversation and unexpected kisses. But like I said, I need a break. And while no one at the campfire would necessarily miss *me*, they would miss the S'mores.

Across the campfire, Victoria spears a marshmallow with a bent coat hanger and holds it over the low flames. I wonder what she thinks, or if she even knows (I hope not), about Sullivan's bizarro lust for me. I don't think there is any official camp "no messing around" rule, but Victoria is pretty protective of Sullivan, always reminding him to put on suntan lotion and eat his greens and zip up his windbreaker on rainy days. I doubt that making out with the "volunteer" help is part of the life plan Victoria has mapped out for Sullivan. She probably thinks he should be kissing teen environmental activists and class representatives. Not…me. Especially not me.

"Storm's coming," Victoria says, waving her flaming marshmallow at the sky.

It's true. The moon disappeared a while ago behind increasingly thick clouds. The headlamps and party lanterns winking from the cabin cruisers out on the river are scattering for shore, a sure sign of troubled weather on the way.

Within minutes the cool evening breeze morphs into a stiff wind. Low, persistent rumbles compete with the crackle of the fire and the smashing of rogue waves on the beach.

At the first flash of lightning and drops of rain, Dr. Fred calls it a night. He douses the fire with a big bucket of river water, and then, without preamble, he strides quickly through the trees and across the field, motioning for everyone else to tag along to the barn. "Storm phobia means canine pandemonium," he remarks.

Joke's on him. Most of the old dogs are curled into themselves on top of blankets or stretched out on their sides on the cool tiles, fast asleep after a day of serious exercise and socializing, oblivious to the electricity in the air and the rain pounding the roof. A few of the younger, inexperienced pups whine and circle around Dr. Fred, looking for no more than head pats and some of the dog treats they know he keeps stuffed in his pants pockets.

Only Judy is a mess, howling and whimpering and quaking with every flash of lightning.

BOOM! The rafters shake. There's another flash. Judy sees me and charges, jumping into my arms like a 130-pound toy poodle. We collapse in a heap.

I push her bulk aside long enough to struggle to my feet. "Come on, Judy," I say, yawning and gesturing for her to follow me, though it isn't necessary; she's got her head stuffed under my armpit like a furry black basketball. We head for the barn door.

"Sarah?" Dr. Fred calls.

"Judy can sleep on the floor in my cabin," I call over my shoulder before making a mad dash through the storm to the cabin cluster. It's so late, I'm so tired, and the storm, while not especially fierce, seems to be stalled over the island. If I stay with Judy here in the barn until the weather clears and the big sucky dog is asleep, I'll never get any rest.

I've never hosted a sleepover before.

I switch on the light in my cabin and take in the small space. There's just enough room to lay out an old blanket for Judy on the floor between the bed and the dresser.

But Judy has other plans. Ten seconds after we reach the cabin, there's another blinding flash of lightning. With a howl and one enormous bound onto the loft bed, Judy wiggles herself under my duvet. Come up and join me, her big shiny eyes plead.

I don't remember Brownie ever talking to me with his eyes and body the way Judy does. He never tried to sleep in my bed either. Not that he'd ever had the opportunity. Dad made Brownie sleep in the garage, even in the winter.

I know Dr. Fred's dog-training books would advise me to reach up and haul Judy off my mattress by her scruff. But I also know that she'd jump right back up with the next flash of lightning. I consider letting Judy take the damn bed and sleeping on the floor myself, but if she were to jump off the loft bed sometime in the night and land on me, I'd be dead. Squashed flat like the Wicked Witch of the East under Dorothy's house. Like dog poo squished under a boot.

Only one thing to do.

I climb up beside Judy, reaching over her to yank the cord that turns off the light. I lie down and squirm around, trying to get comfortable. Lightning flashes again and Judy pushes up against me, whimpering. There's room for both of us on the narrow bunk, but just barely.

Loud rumbles continue, shaking my flimsy cabin walls like a minor earthquake, for a good half hour more, but as the lightning diminishes, Judy settles. Her fur smells of dirt and grass despite all her swimming. Her feet smell like nacho-cheese Doritos. Judy sticks out her juicy tongue and licks my cheek, panting hot, kibble-scented breath in my face and nuzzling her wet nose into my neck. "Thank you," she seems to be saying, as if I am personally responsible for sending the storm packing.

If only I had that much control over her life. Or my own.

Great. Judy snores. I'll never get to sleep.

This time, the joke's on me. Cramped in that loft bed, overheated by a giant fur ball who refuses to budge, fur tickling my nose, damp doggie breath polluting the air, I sleep. Deeply. Dreaming of toasted marshmallows, guitar music, cool breezes and warm wet kisses.

Weird.

SEVENTEEN

After lunch cleanup a few days later, I'm down on the beach with Judy, taking my so-called afternoon break. It's quiet out on the channel today. A few freighters chug along in the distance, but there's not a tourist boat in sight. Gentle waves lap at the shore with a sound like little dogs lapping water from their bowls.

Judy is stretched out in the cool gravel beside me. She's been bounding in and out of the river for the past half hour, chasing sticks and seagulls. Finally she's ready to take a break too. Catch a few dog zzzzzz's.

Footsteps crunch toward us along the beach path. Sullivan plunks down on my other side. "You okay?" he asks me, kicking off his high-tops—purple polka-dots today—and digging his toes into the gravel.

I toss him what I hope is an "everything's peachy" grin, but it feels strained and lopsided, more like a sneer or grimace. "Why wouldn't I be?"

Sullivan frowns. He hunches over and starts piling small rocks, flat and smooth from years of river erosion, one on top of another until his structure collapses. "You were so quiet at lunch."

I snort. "Nicky and Brant were talking enough for all of us."

"Ah, they were just joking around," Sullivan says, lying back on the beach, resting his palms behind his head.

Something hot and sour pools at the back of my throat. "What's so fucking funny about having your bare-assed baby pictures passed around the table like they're a bowl of potato salad?" I snarl. Little drops of spit fly out of my mouth.

Sullivan sits up and laughs. "Not *my* fault. Nicholas found one of Mom's old photo albums on the bookshelf in the rec room."

"Didn't you even…mind?"

"Mind what?"

I blink hard. "Mind that everyone could see your bare ass!"

Sullivan cranes his neck down and around in a goofy attempt to check out his own backside. "Why would I?" he replies, grinning. "I have a nice ass. Didn't your family ever take any bare-assed baby photos of you?"

I grab a big rock off the beach, wishing it were a grenade, except it's me that might explode. I toss it far out into the river, where it lands with a loud *KERPLOP*.

Sullivan reaches over and squeezes my shoulder. "Don't be such a prude," he snickers.

"I'm not a prude."

"Then I guess suggesting a round of strip poker tonight wouldn't be out of the question?" Sullivan asks, his eyes bright with amusement.

Just ignore him, just ignore him, just ignore him, I tell myself.

"No? Maybe we could listen to a few Barenaked Ladies CDs?"

I suck air in, holding my breath as long as I can, waiting for the earth to open up and suck me down into the dirt.

"Sarah?"

"I thought you wanted to work on the puzzle tonight, Sullivan!" I growl. "Or would you rather not? Because it's your damn puzzle. I don't care if—" I stop, because I do care. No puzzle, no concert. No concert, no treasure hunt for me. "Sorry," I mumble, because I am. I really wish I could laugh as easily as Sullivan does about being the "butt" of Brant's and Nicky's jokes.

Sullivan raises an eyebrow at me and lets out a low whistle. "Wow…are you ever an Oscar today."

"What the hell are you talking about now?"

"An Oscar. You know? *Sesame Street*? Oscar the *Grouch*."

I'd leave now, but I don't have the heart to rouse Judy, who's snoring away, her soft black ears flapping in the breeze. "Aren't you supposed to be hosing out the barn this afternoon?" I ask Sullivan. Maybe he'll take the hint and leave me alone.

"Actually…Mom sent me to check on you." Sullivan blushes.

Figures. "Victoria worries too much."

"It's a refreshing change for her to be worried about someone other than me."

"What's she got to worry about you for?" I ask. I'm curious because Sullivan seems to me like the poster boy for normalcy, if you can get past his weird shoe fetish, his motormouth and his thing for me. And if I can get him talking about himself, maybe he'll stop pestering me with questions.

Sullivan takes in a long breath and chews on his lip. His expression reminds me of that day in the canoe, when I'd asked him a similar question about Victoria's over-protectiveness, and he'd told me to watch out for a nonexistent piece of driftwood.

But he doesn't hedge this time. "Well, you might as well know, seeing we're…you know…friends. I had cancer. Leukemia."

I blink hard. "You did?"

Sullivan draws a tic-tac-toe board in the dirt with his finger. "First grade. With Mrs. Fenton. Don't you remember?"

"You were in first grade with me?"

He draws an X in the center square, solemn now. "We shared a glue stick in arts and crafts."

"No. I always shared a glue stick with a kid named Steve." Steve had thick, curly brown hair, a Ninja Turtle lunch box, and Disney Band-Aids on his knees and elbows almost all the time. He got a bloody nose—a real gusher—one day. The class was making Thanksgiving turkeys out of brown lunch bags and construction paper. I remember because Steve dripped blood on my turkey. Mike Kindale got jealous. He said the blood made my turkey look like "a real turkey just after my daddy's shot it." He wanted Steve to bleed on his paper-bag turkey too, but Mrs. Fenton rushed Steve to the office for first aid instead.

Steve never came back.

Except, it turns out, he did. Sullivan laughs. "Steve was a nickname. Short for STV. Sullivan Thomas Vickerson is too big a mouthful for any six-year-old kid." He nudges me and motions down to his tic-tac-toe board. "Your turn."

I draw an O in the top left corner. "That was *you*? God. I'm sorry. Wow."

"Yeah, I didn't make it back to school until—"

"Grade two." It's all coming back now. "We had Mr. Baldwin." I was sharing glue sticks with a girl named Sylvia by then, so I'd barely noticed the skinny "new boy" with thin spiky hair and a Scooby Doo lunch box. The boy who went by the name Sullivan.

I peer at him now through my hair. He looks healthy enough to star in a breakfast cereal commercial. "You really had cancer? You're okay now, right?"

Sullivan shrugs and puts an X in the bottom right corner. "It's been almost ten years since my last treatment. I went into remission ahead of schedule. Never had a relapse. Probably never will. Dr. Walters says I'm one of those few lucky kids who breeze through cancer—if you can get past the unluckiness of getting cancer at all.

But tell that to my mother. If I get the sniffles or a hangnail or even just a headache, there's Mom, standing vigil. Usually by the phone, since I'm with Dad most of the year."

"Your dad's cool about it, isn't he?" Besides ninth-grade homeroom, I'd had Mr. Vickerson for physical geography just last semester. He was a fair marker. He prepared interesting slide shows and took us on field trips to the nearby provincial park. He always wrote a cornball "joke of the day" on the board before the start of classes.

Sullivan chuckles. "Sure, he's cool. But he's *everywhere*. At school, my locker and his office are less than ten paces apart. Dad's not the hovering type. He's not at all restrictive. But he's…watchful. Like, if he misses one of my volleyball games or a drama club play or even just turns his attention elsewhere for a minute, he thinks I'm going to break out in tumors. Take your turn."

I put an O in the top right corner. If I know anything, I know what it's like to have a parent who can't keep his distance.

"But you know, Sarah," Sullivan adds, quickly drawing an X in the top center square to block my win, "there's an upside to having cancer too." He rests his weight back on his hands, tilting his face up to the sun.

"Let me guess. Spoiled rotten?"

Sullivan sits back up and counts off on his fingers. "Disney World trips during elementary school. Karate and drama and soccer and drum lessons through junior high. My dad promised me a car for my high school graduation. One with a spotless safety rating, of course."

I draw an O in the bottom center box. Game over. Tied. "None of that explains why they let you spend your summer hanging with juvies."

"I live with my mother in the summer. My mother lives here in the summer. Besides, both my parents know that none of you 'volunteers' would have been sent here if you were real...you know..."

"Criminals?"

"You aren't a criminal, Sarah."

"Sullivan, I stole a car and crashed it into a war monument. I was underage, without a license. Isn't that reason enough to red flag me as a questionable...friend?"

"Don't be so hard on yourself. I mean, that night you crashed? It was all just an accident, right? An impulsive moment?"

Same as with my mother, it's easiest for me to just let Sullivan think whatever he wants. Let him assume that the actions that landed me at Camp Dog Gone Fun were just a one-off, maybe a fight with my mother about getting a nose ring. Or a bad reaction to Mom's growing relationship with Tanner. Normal teenage hysteria gone overboard. Gone wrong.

"Anyway," Sullivan says, picking pebbles out of his heels, "what does any of it matter as long as whatever happened is worked out now. It is worked out now, right?"

"Sure, Sullivan." Whatever you say.

"Good," he says, and he leans over to kiss me.

It's weird. Until that first kiss in the boathouse a while back, I always worried that, after years of being watched, but never touched, I'd freak if anyone ever *did* touch me. I worried that a kiss would be like a photograph, something to be taken from me.

But it seems I worried for nothing. Sullivan gives kisses; he doesn't steal them.

In fact, kissing seems to be as good a diversion as any from Sullivan's nosy questions. Another bonus: I notice that Sullivan keeps his eyes shut tight while he kisses me; he's no pervert who needs to watch. Doesn't a guy deserve points if he's willing to kiss a girl he knows is covered in dog hair and drool?

"Maybe sharing a glue stick back in first grade was just the start of something," Sullivan remarks when we break for air.

"Maybe." But what sort of something, I wonder. And I don't want to know. I've been trying so hard to ignore the white-water river of electricity that runs through me when Sullivan kisses me. Because, realistically, how much of myself can I actually share with him? Even if I didn't have secret motives for agreeing to help him with his puzzle, at what point would my past interfere?

Never mind about all that now, I tell myself. Concentrate on Sullivan tickling your upper lip with his tongue. Enjoy this while you can. Until the Ratgut concert, when you ditch him at the gates to go picture hunting, and he never kisses you, never speaks to you, again.

That's the plan.

I'm such a bitch. I'd never use Sullivan—use anyone, even creepy Brant—like this if finding the Polaroids wasn't the only thing that really mattered in my life.

Judy lumbers to her feet, stretches and shakes half the beach from her thick coat all over us. Sullivan and I recoil, laughing and jumping up, shaking gravel from our own hair and spitting dirt onto the beach.

All three of us plunk back down on the beach to recuperate. "So…want to make it official?" Sullivan asks, nudging me playfully in the ribs. "Want to be my girlfriend?"

I run my fingers through Judy's damp tail hair, untangling it to prevent mats, and turn Sullivan's question over—and over and over, like a dozen sizzling blueberry pancakes—in my mind. Maybe I could handle it, being someone's girlfriend. Short-term, obviously. Sort of like a social science experiment. Romance with an expiration date.

"You mean just for the summer, right?" I play along, knowing already it can only last until the second Saturday in August.

"Well…no," Sullivan says. "I was hoping…well, maybe it's a little premature to say *forever*, but for…as long as it lasts?"

"What? You mean like even through the school year?"

He can't be serious. I might be his only choice out on Moose Island (Johanna is very "taken" by a beefy senior quarterback, and Taylor's latest poem was called "Lesbian Love Lessons"), but how could I possibly compete with the entire female population of Riverwood High School once school starts back in September? And what would I do if Sullivan—if any guy—asked me to a school dance? Everyone gets pictures taken at school dances. The Riverwood yearbook photographers stalk new couples like paparazzi.

"Why not through the school year?" Sullivan's eyes, usually flashing humor and enthusiasm, are suddenly seeping with hurt. His nose and his ears turn purplish red, like the beet casserole my father used to make at Christmas. "Sarah, don't you *know*?"

"Know what?"

"I've…uh…liked you…for…um…years," he stammers.

My mouth drops open. All I can think of to say is "Why?" I wonder if Sullivan has some sort of bizarre, flawed ESP that detects something in me that transcends all the damage and all my rage. Something I've never detected in myself.

"I used to see you in the school library," Sullivan says, pouting a little now. I fight off a demented urge to lean over and bite his protruding bottom lip. "I always wanted to go over and talk to you."

"Why didn't you?"

"Your face was always hidden behind a novel. What were you reading, anyway? Thrillers? Classics?"

I give an embarrassed shrug. "Just girly shit. *The Princess Diaries. Gossip Girls.*"

I really don't think Sullivan needs to know how greedily I devoured those glossy novels about rich girls trolling for boys and fighting over prom dresses. How captivated I was by their stupid social dilemmas. I envied their worlds, where problems with boys and nails and hairstyles wrapped up neatly by *The End* and everyone lived happily (and expensively) ever after. In my experience, *The End* wasn't the end at all.

I also don't think Sullivan wants to know that spending my lunch hours and spares in the school library has never had anything to do with me having an obsessive love of reading. It has everything to do with avoiding the noon clubs and sports teams and cafeteria cliques that inevitably lead to "Say cheese, Sarah! Smile for the yearbook picture!"

Sullivan reaches over and scratches Judy behind the ears. He watches my face, his own eager and puppy-like, still waiting for my final answer to his girlfriend question.

When I can't stand the being-gawked-at feeling any longer, I shriek, "Yes! I'll be your girlfriend! Just stop staring at me!"

Sullivan grins. "I always liked your eyes, Sarah. They're so dark and intense, like you have a million secrets."

"Don't go there, Sullivan." Without my secrets I'd be as hollow as a chocolate Easter bunny.

But Sullivan keeps right on yapping like a Yorkie, oblivious to my discomfort. "I've seen you around school for so many years now. But I can't really say I've ever gotten to know you. Not before this summer, anyway. You know why I think you landed out here at Moose Island this summer, Sarah? I think it was...fate."

What an idiot.

"You want to know what I like best about you, Sarah?"

Pass.

"You make the best chocolate chip cookies I've ever eaten."

Okay. That is news I can handle.

E I G H T E E N

Ten minutes after Sullivan leaves to start his afternoon chores, I'm summoned away from the beach.

"Sarah! Sar—*SQUAWK*—ah! Please—*SQUAWK*—report to the—*SQUAWK*—barn!"

I jump up, gather Judy and my belongings together and rush up the path and across the field to the barn.

Dr. Fred greets us at the door, half a lime Popsicle sticking out of his mouth. He offers the other half to me, then pulls a pork roll out of his pocket and tosses it to Judy. She catches it in her mouth and trots off with it to the shady side of the barn.

"Am I in trouble?" I ask. Being summoned over the intercom means that the problem can't wait until dinner.

"Of course not!" Dr. Fred laughs. "Quite the contrary! I have a great honor to bestow on you! Well...a great favor to ask you. No pressure, of course."

I suck on my Popsicle and wait for him to tell me what he wants. He's not my father, so whatever it is, it can't be that bad.

Dr. Fred cracks his knuckles. "Would you take charge of cooking for the Dog Daze Festival."

"The *what* Festival?"

"The Dog Daze Festival is Camp Dog Gone Fun's annual open house. I invite reps from all the different service clubs that have donated cash or equipment to our program to come out for a day of mixing and mingling. It's good for our donors to see their money being well spent." He chuckles. "They may even feel compelled to donate more."

"When is this…festival?"

"This coming weekend. Saturday afternoon."

"And how many people are coming?"

"Hmm…oh…two hundred…or so."

A chunk of Popsicle breaks off the stick and slides down my throat whole. After I've finished choking, I sputter. "You want me to cater a picnic for two *hundred* people? This weekend?"

Dr. Fred laughs. "I usually bring someone over from town to barbecue burgers and throw together a potato salad. Maybe cut up a watermelon and put out a few bowls of chips. This is a dog camp, after all, not the prime minister's mansion. But my regular caterer just called to say he has food poisoning. So I thought of you."

I take a deep breath. "I can flip a few burgers, I guess."

"Actually," Dr. Fred says, "I was hoping to get away from the barbecued food this summer. Too many hazards with the dogs circling the grills. Not good for business to have an accident with all the media types around."

His praise is lost on me. Something heavy and hairy, tarantula-like, begins crawling around the pit of my stomach. "Media types?"

"There are half a dozen reporters who always show up," Dr. Fred replies. "Cute dog photos sell papers."

"Great," I say, biting so hard into my Popsicle stick that a splinter pierces my cheek.

Dr. Fred is too happy to notice my cringing. "Anyway, about the food. I thought that a big vat of your terrific homemade chili would be just what we need to replace the burgers. Plus a few salads, a fruit plate, a couple of desserts. Would you do it, Sarah?"

"Will I have to spend all day in the kitchen?"

"Well…probably. But maybe Victoria could help?" Dr. Fred ponders. "So you could take a break? I'd help you out myself if I had any talent at that sort of—"

I suck in a deep breath of relief. Never have two lungs full of smog felt so fresh.

"Dr. Fred?"

"Yeah."

"I'll do it. All of it. *So* not a problem."

Dr. Fred lights up like the sun. "Thanks, Sarah!" He tosses his Popsicle stick into a nearby wastebasket and hugs me. A short, enthusiastic, grateful squeeze.

What those cheerful teen novels might describe as a fatherly hug.

So that's what it feels like.

NINETEEN

"Too hard," Sullivan mutters. He and I are having a contest to see who can put the most pieces into the German shepherd puzzle before 11:00 PM—the bedtime Victoria imposes on everyone at Camp Dog Gone Fun.

I am ahead by twenty-three pieces tonight.

Make that twenty-four.

"Yes!" I shout as another piece of the German shepherd's face falls into place. I glance up to gloat at Sullivan. And know instantly why his progress tonight has been so poor.

"What the hell are you staring at?" I shout.

As if I don't know. Bent over, distracted by the puzzle and my desire to kick Sullivan's ass at the jigsaw, I didn't realize that the neck of my baggy T-shirt is hanging down, giving Sullivan an eyeful. I yank at my shirt and straighten up.

"Sorry," he says sheepishly.

"I'm done here," I announce.

Sullivan pries his eyes away from me long enough to steal a glance at his watch. "You're right. It's past ten thirty. No way I can beat your score now. You win, Sarah. But tomorrow, just you wait. I'll—"

I wave my hand over the puzzle, fighting off a red-raged impulse to upend the whole table. "No, Sullivan. I'm done. Done helping you with the puzzle."

Except I already know I don't mean it. Because then I'll have to figure out some other way to get into the city this summer. Maybe I could "borrow" a canoe and paddle it over to the mainland in the dead of night. Hitchhike to the city.

Yeah, stupid, a voice in my head asserts. *And end up finishing high school in juvenile detention. Or drowned. Or raped. Or murdered.*

Outside, doors slam as people head to their cabins. Victoria has taken to blasting some new-agey CD over the intercom to bore everyone into bed each evening.

Nicholas passes under the light by the shed's screen door, huffing and puffing as he drags the Camp Dog Gone Fun slop buckets behind him. He drew the Waste Management straw at flagpole this morning; it's his job to feed the day's veggie peels and table scraps to the enormous composter across the field. "Badass mosquitoes," he grumbles. "I'm gonna catch West Nile disease and die."

"Sarah? Why are you so pissed at me?" Sullivan pokes my arm.

"You were looking down my shirt!" I hiss, yanking my arm away.

"I was not!" he lies, his face distorting painfully as he tries not to laugh. "Is it okay if I look at your eyebrows?"

"My what?"

He reaches out and traces them with his finger and wiggles his own to make the point. "Your eyebrows do this weird thing when you're pissed off. One goes up, one goes down. I've seen you do it when Brant calls you Sarah-ha-ha too. You're going to have some seriously bizarre wrinkles when you're forty if you don't lighten up."

"Bye." I turn to pull open the shed door. I'll have to take my chances escaping Camp Dog Gone Fun on my own. Sarah Greene, fugitive. Nice ring to it.

But Sullivan blocks my way. He gets down on one knee and reaches for my hand. "Sarah, will you puh-leeese forgive me for being a horny teenage guy? Puh-leeese keep helping me with the puzzle?"

He's not getting off the hook that easily. "Will you stop trying to look down my shirt?"

"Absolutely."

"You promise?"

"I promise. For you, Sarah...anything." Sullivan gets up and walks over to the puzzle table. "You're good at this stuff, Sarah," he says, jabbing a finger at the German shepherd's nose. "Maybe I need glasses."

Here's the thing: if Sullivan were blind, he'd be the perfect boyfriend.

Sullivan is already a good boyfriend, a nagging voice inside me says. *It's you, Sarah, who has the problem.*

"If you desert me now, Sarah," Sullivan continues, "I'll have to finish this puzzle on my own. It'll take a year, at least. We won't just miss the Ratgut concert. I'll miss school in September." He sticks his bottom lip out. "I'll miss... Christmas."

"Sullivan, enough of the drama club audition, already."

"So you'll help me?"

I help you, you help me. That's the plan. "Yeah, I guess."

"Thank you! Thank you! Thank you! Come on, Sarah!" Sullivan tugs playfully at my arm. "We've got another twenty minutes before Mom lets out the border collies to herd us to bed." He grabs my hand and leads me back to the puzzle. "Let's see if we can get the other ear filled in before—"

The shed is plunged into total darkness.

"What the hell?"

"Power's out," Sullivan grumbles.

I feel my way to the screen door. A pale moon struggles to cut through the smog. "Why? There's no storm."

"This happens a few times every summer," Sullivan explains. "Humid nights like tonight, too many people on the mainland crank up their air conditioners at the same time."

"So what are we supposed to do now?"

"Nothing. Wait it out."

"Will the dogs be okay?"

"Sure. There's a generator behind the barn that powers up the necessities: the kennel equipment, the kitchen appliances, the emergency lights."

Footsteps and a strong light beam invade the eerie darkness outside the shed.

"Here comes Luke Skywalker," Sullivan whispers.

He's not kidding. Dr. Fred, wielding a three-foot light saber, is banging on cabin doors and handing out flashlights. From the shed's doorway, I watch him, cast in a lime green aura, circle the barn and check the generator box, jiggling switches and letting out a triumphant "TA-DA!" as the lodge and barn light up like Christmas trees.

Continuing on his rounds, Dr. Fred stops by the storage shed. Sullivan and I are still inside in the dark. "Everything okay in here?" he asks, passing me a flashlight. "Need an escort back to your cabin, Sarah? I'm heading your way."

"We've still got a few minutes, Doc," Sullivan pipes up. He pulls his cell phone out of his pocket to check the time. "Maybe the power will come back on quickly. Ten more minutes. We won't miss curfew."

Dr. Fred pats my arm, then winks—*winks!*—at Sullivan. "That puzzle sure means a lot to you two, eh?" he laughs, waggling his light saber at us as he scurries off to rescue Nicholas, who is cursing as he tries to pry off the composter lid in the dark.

"Dr. Fred thinks we're in here making out," I hiss at Sullivan.

"So?" He wraps his arms around me in the dark, his body warm and dry and clean-smelling, like a flannel blanket.

We stumble over to the stack of old gym mats piled at the back of the shed. They get dragged out during the day to provide some of the older dogs a softer place to lie than the pebbly ground.

Sullivan's lips fumble around my face until they find my mouth.

His fingers grope under my T-shirt.

I reach down and grab his wrists, knowing this is the part where I'm supposed to wrench his hands away. Instead I nudge them higher.

Minutes later I'm running my hands through Sullivan's spiky hair. His face is buried in my chest. I feel carefree, like I'm on vacation. No worries. And Sullivan may not be a world-class ball player the way Brant professes to be, but he sure knows how to make the most of second base.

Until the lights burst back on.

"Stop staring at me!" I shout, shoving him away from me.

"I'm not," Sullivan laughs, putting his hands in front of his eyes and peering through his fingers as I struggle to sort out my bra and pull my shirt down.

I push him off and struggle to sit up. "You are so!"

"Sarah, you're like the opposite of those *Look, Don't Touch* signs you see in antique stores."

"What the hell are you talking about?"

"If you had a sign it would say *Touch, Don't Look*. You could get it tattooed across your chest. In Braille," he snorts.

"Very fucking funny."

"I'm your boyfriend, Sarah. Why are you so weird about—"

"I'm not weird." Who am I kidding? "Okay…maybe I am weird. So what?"

Sullivan gestures to the jigsaw puzzle. "You're harder to piece together than Rover."

"Good." If I have anything to say about it, Sullivan will never sort out the Sarah puzzle. Even I don't know what the finished puzzle looks like anymore.

"Is that why you avoid people at school?" Sullivan asks.

Where did that come from? "I don't avoid people. There are people in the library."

"Yeah, but they're studying. I never see you talking to people."

"People ask too many questions."

"Do I ask too many questions?" Sullivan's watch beeps eleven.

"We've got to go." I push open the screen door. "Nighty-night," I call; then I sprint toward my cabin across the field.

I hear Sullivan secure the door latch and run the other way, toward the lodge. I can't help it. I stop to watch him racing through the moonlight. He's so tame, but he moves like a cheetah.

He glances over his shoulder and catches me watching him, almost as if he knew I would be.

Then Sullivan raises his index and middle fingers in a peace sign and yells out one of Humphrey Bogart's lines from that old movie, *Casablanca*. We watched it in the ninth-grade film studies elective.

"Here's looking at you, kid."

TWENTY

"Testing, testing...*SQUAWK*...Today's the big day!!!... *SQUAWK*...My favorite day of the...*SQUAWK*...year!!!"

I'd been hoping for rain. Or hail. Or a plague of locusts. A global-warming catastrophe. Anything to cancel what Dr. Fred is calling his favorite day of the year.

So much for praying for an environmental disaster. The weather today is glorious. Blue sky, balmy air and just enough breeze to blow the bugs, smog and doggy smell downriver.

And like the weather, I wake up fine. No chicken pox to keep me quarantined in my cabin. No pinkeye or poison ivy to segregate me from the masses. No headaches, no rashes, no cramps even. I am the goddamn picture of health.

According to Dr. Fred, we're expecting everyone he knows to attend: townspeople, past donors, potential donors, people who adopted pets from his clinic in town, newspaper reporters and (aggggh!) photographers from all the little towns along this stretch of the St. Lawrence.

And everyone's dogs too.

I intend to spend all day in the kitchen hiding behind the pots and pans.

While I wash my hands at the kitchen sink, I run through the day's menu in my head. I had prepared an enormous cauldron of chili last night. I still need to make chicken salad, a sweet potato salad, two kinds of coleslaw and a tossed salad with spinach and cherry tomatoes.

I also have to squeeze lemons for the lemonade, brew tea for the iced tea, blend the fruit smoothies, slice the veggies, mix the dips, cut the cheese, lay out the crackers and defrost three different desserts: chocolate brownies, apple tarts and oatmeal cookies.

And that's just for the two-legged guests.

For the dogs, I've already made an assortment of treats: chicken and cheese nibbles; sesame seed and molasses morsels; mixed-vegetable muffins with beef glaze; and Judy's new favorite, peanut butter bones. And I've jotted down the details for an extra-special iced and decorated birthday cake for Trixie the beagle, Camp Dog Gone Fun's oldest camper ever. The old girl just turned eighteen. The actual cake will be a blend of oatmeal, ground beef, eggs and brown rice baked in a springform pan, with icing made from a large can of Eukanuba Senior, blended until smooth and spreadable. Decorations will include hot dog slices and carrot shavings. It will take me about an hour to prepare and about forty-five seconds for Trixie and her pack of canine buddies to devour every last scrap of it.

By midafternoon, the island is a zoo. Worse than a zoo, because there are no barricades to keep the visitors at a respectable distance.

The Moose Island dog population has tripled with all the canine visitors, and, as Dr. Fred predicted, a couple of hundred humans are milling around on the field, vying for shade, many armed with cameras or video recorders.

Shuddering, I back away from the window, preferring the company of the oven, the stove and Judy (who was banished from the field midmorning after tackling and upending the port-a-potty Dr. Fred had rented for the day. Brant was inside at the time, ha ha). Victoria, Taylor and Nicholas have all offered to help with the cooking so I can take a break, but I send them back out to work the crowd with trays of food.

I am up to my elbows—literally—in dog biscuit batter (we'd already run out of all my pre-made biscuits) when Dr. Fred rushes into the kitchen through the screen door, a strange woman in tow.

"Well, aren't you a big doggie!" The woman makes a beeline for Judy, who is tied to the table leg to prevent her from jumping onto the counter after brownies and cinnamon rolls. The woman is treated to a tongue bath and is hip-checked into a chair.

To her credit, the woman laughs. Uproariously. "And so friendly!" she gushes, giving Judy's haunches a good rub.

"Sarah, this is Helen Minter!" Dr. Fred exclaims, as if Helen Minter is a movie star or a politician. Someone I should know.

Helen smiles broadly and extends a right hand worthy of a lotion commercial: perfectly soft skin, long fingers and shiny unchipped polish on manicured nails that probably cost her over a hundred bucks a month to maintain.

I glance down at my own right hand, at the worthy-of-a-horror-movie chapped skin and chewed-down nails covered in grayish brown biscuit batter. I quickly rinse my hands under the tap, wipe them dry on my shorts and extend one to Helen.

Dr. Fred is bouncing up and down on the balls of his feet, trembling like a puppy, so excited I wonder if he's going to pee right there on the kitchen floor.

"Helen is an old friend of mine, Sarah," he says. "We went to high school together up in Cornwall. She lives in Toronto now, but she's been spending a few weeks with friends upriver, at Wolfe Island. They brought their boat—and their dogs—down to check out the fun today."

"I'm a *huge* dog lover," Helen gushes. "I have two Jack Russells and a cocker—"

"Uh, excuse me," I interrupt, sniffing the air. The peanut butter bones will start burning in exactly ten seconds. I grab an oven mitt off the counter, stick my hand in the oven, extract the tray of dog cookies, set it on top of the counter, grab a fresh tray of unbaked biscuits, shove it into the oven and slam the door shut. All in one fluid movement, like my own private culinary ballet.

I look up and Dr. Fred and Helen are still there, smiling at me benevolently.

"Helen's a holistic pet-food manufacturer, Sarah," Dr. Fred says. "Tricks for Treats, Inc."

"How would you like to have your dog biscuits mass-produced and marketed all over Ontario?" Helen asks.

Is she talking to me? Several strands of hair have fallen out of my ponytail into my eyes. I peer at Helen through them. The woman can't be serious.

Except she is. "Let me explain. Dr. Fred tells me you are quite the chef. More importantly, he was telling me how you've been experimenting with dog biscuit recipes. My own dogs are out there gorging on your creations as we speak. And, well…" She leans toward me and whispers, "They looked so tasty I even nibbled on a few myself."

So that's why the biscuits disappeared so fast. The humans were eating them. "You want to buy my recipes?" I ask.

Helen nods. "Dr. Fred would be willing to endorse the final product, of course. He tells me you've been reading up on pet nutrition in your spare time and clearing all your ingredients with him before you bake. It's essential that you don't use food items that would jeopardize the dogs' health."

I nod. "Like chocolate and onions."

Helen continues. "What I'm especially taken with is your presentation. It's quite clever, Sarah, using cookie cutters to make festive shapes, cornmeal sprinkles for texture and veggie puree for color."

"The dogs don't really care about all that," I admit, waving a stray fly away from the tray of dog biscuits cooling on the counter.

"No," Helen agrees, "but their owners do. Think about all those companies that sell designer dog coats. They make a killing. Dogs don't give a hoot if their cold-weather gear is blue or red, or made of wool or denim, as long as it keeps them warm. But the dog *owners* buy the coats, not the dogs."

"You have to market to the owners," Dr. Fred pipes up.

"And owners like shapes and sprinkles and colors," I say, catching on.

"Exactly!" Helen gushes. "So how about it, Sarah?"

"I...wow..." I feel like I'm standing on a rising loaf of bread.

Dr. Fred pulls out chairs. "Here, ladies. Let's sit." He yanks open the fridge door and pulls out a pitcher. "Lemonade?" he asks Helen.

"Sure."

"Sarah?" He offers me a glass.

I look frantically around the kitchen. "I guess I could take a short break," I say, slowly lowering myself into a chair.

"I know this must seem a bit overwhelming," Helen says to me kindly. "But it will be a while, a year *at least*, before you'll actually see your products on the shelves of the big-box pet stores."

How would my father feel about me landing this deal? And so easily. Without ever asking for it. Without even thinking it was something I might want to do someday.

Here's the thing: if the dead can really see the living, I'd so much rather my father be sickly green with envy right now than rosy with the glow of fatherly pride. Except that my father was never the jealous type. He'd be happy for me. Ecstatic. Pleased as rum-spiked punch.

Helen takes a sip of lemonade and continues, "I always have someone do market testing before I commit to full-scale production of new products, so I can't offer you much up front. Would two thousand be okay?"

DOLLARS? That was more money than I'd make in a *year* serving coffee and crullers part-time at the Doughy Donut Emporium.

"Um...sure...that would be great," I admit. "But... uh...can I ask you a question?"

"Of course."

I take a deep breath and glance up through my hair at Helen. "Would you need to take photographs?"

She smiles. "Of course! Visuals are very important. I'll even bring in a food stylist to work with the photographer to make sure all photos of the finished biscuits look both professionally baked and—more importantly—mouth-watering."

"I like it!" I exclaim. Anything that doesn't involve taking my photograph is fine with me.

Judy barks.

"Sarah, I'm so proud of you!" Dr. Fred interjects, reaching across the table to squeeze my arm.

He is proud of me. I can tell. And Dr. Fred's pride means way more to me than knowing my father would be proud. Because Dr. Fred's pride is so…uncomplicated.

Helen looks at her watch. "Yikes, it's getting late. My friends and I have to be pushing off. We're doing dinner in town this evening." She grabs her purse off the back of her chair and rummages around inside. Extracting a business card and extending it to me, she says, "How about you spend the rest of the summer perfecting a set of recipes? Ten to fifteen should be plenty. We'll choose a few to start with."

"Works for me."

"I'll be back at my office in Toronto in two weeks. I'll draft a contract and have my assistant send it to your home address." She locates a notepad in her purse, rips off a piece of paper and passes me a pen so I can write it down for her. "You'll want to have a parent look over the contract, maybe hire a lawyer to—"

"I…uh…already have a lawyer," I mention, scribbling my Riverwood address on the paper and passing it back to Helen.

"That's…handy," she muses, a grimace of concern flashing across her face for a nanosecond. Dr. Fred introduces all his community service teens as "volunteers," so Helen may not know she just offered a contract to a juvenile offender.

I'm feeling a bit giddy, like Dr. Fred spiked my lemonade, though fat chance he did. "Just don't ask me to write any driving manuals," I add, giggling.

"Yes. Well, then, Sarah," Helen says, extending her hand once again. "I'll be in touch."

Dr. Fred leaves to walk Helen back to the dock. When both are out of sight, I bound over to Judy and bury my face in her fur. Judy licks my ear. Dog drool seeps down my neck. "My recipes are going to be *famous*, Judy," I whisper, ignoring the strands of dog hair poking their way into my mouth. Outside the kitchen window, through the loud buzz of the crowd, I can hear Sullivan laughing about something. "And I have a boyfriend, Judy. For a couple more weeks, anyway."

Judy wiggles around happily, slurping my cheek.

I laugh. "And yes, you big hairball. I have you too."

This is supposed to be my summer of punishment. What a joke.

Except the day's not over.

TWENTY-ONE

The day has been a huge success. Lots of sunshine. Lots of food. Oodles of Frisbee flying, good-natured barking and laughter. And the happy *ka-ching* of cash donations for the Camp Dog Gone Fun program. Dr. Fred is beaming.

By seven thirty, most of the dog-loving crowds have packed up and headed home. As I gear up to wash the final load of dirty serving bowls, I breathe a huge sigh of relief.

Until the mayor of Gananoque, Dr. Fred's only no-show, decides to show up after all.

He pulls up to the dock in a cabin cruiser. Gawking out the open kitchen window, I see him pumping Dr. Fred's hand. As they cross the field to the lodge, the mayor, in a booming voice that carries across the island, apologizes for coming so late; he'd been tied up at a Girl Guide barbecue for the homeless.

"You think it was the Girl Guides or the homeless that tied him up?" Taylor whispers. She's standing on the porch with Brant and Nicholas and Johanna, divvying up grounds-cleanup duties. I can hear them all clearly through the screen door.

"I wouldn't mind being tied up by a pack of Girl Guides." Brant leers.

"You think the mayor brought any Girl Guide cookies with him?" Nicholas wonders.

"He's kind of cute," Johanna says. I peek out the window and watch as she sashays down the porch steps and over to the mayor, swinging her hips in tight pink sweatpants with *HOT! HOT! HOT!* spelled out across the ass in glitter letters. She'd probably let the mayor tie *her* up if it would get her off Moose Island for the rest of the summer. She's had to do Poo Patrol the past eleven days in a row.

The mayor has come to Camp Dog Gone Fun with one of those oversized checks you see on telethons and lottery commercials. Enough cash for Dr. Fred to attack some much-needed renovations to the camp.

Mr. Mayor also has an entourage with him—a reporter and a photographer from the *St. Lawrence Livewire*, a regional gossip rag.

And they don't just want a photo of Dr. Fred grinning with gratitude beside a few of the old dogs wagging their tails with glee as the mayor presents his check. No, they want a big group shot. They want Dr. Fred and Victoria and Sullivan and all of the Camp Dog Gone Fun "volunteers" and all twenty-three dogs huddled together like a hockey team after winning the Stanley Cup.

I toss Judy a worried glance and wonder if the two of us have time to make a run for it. Maybe we could dash upstairs and hide under Sullivan's bed until the mayor leaves the island. No, Judy won't fit. Maybe we could—

"Sarah! Come on out!" Sullivan yells through the screen door at me. "The mayor wants a picture. We'll be on the front page of the paper tomorrow!"

I wave a soapy yellow rubber glove at him. "Sorry. Busy."

Sullivan opens the screen door and pokes his head in. "We can wait a few minutes." He spies a plate of leftover brownies, grabs one and stuffs it into his mouth.

"No. Seriously, Sullivan. Go ahead without me," I insist, nudging him back toward the door. Stealing a glance out the screen door, I see the photographer attach an elaborate flash to his camera and screw the whole works onto a tripod.

Sullivan swallows. "Come on, Sarah," he chides, brushing brownie crumbs off his shorts.

"Can't." I gesture to Judy sprawled on the kitchen floor like a bear rug, one sleepy eye closed after an afternoon of taste testing and trying to stay out of trouble, the other eye wide open, still keen to what's going on around her. "She's...resting."

Sullivan wipes brownie crumbs off his mouth with his shirtsleeve. "So leave her where she is."

I take off the yellow gloves and set them by the sink. I feel ridiculous arguing with them on, like I'm starring in a dish-liquid commercial. "She'll break the table if I leave her. It's not very sturdy. And she'll eat all the leftover cinnamon rolls. They're for breakfast tomorrow."

"So lock her in the bathroom upstairs."

"Sarah! Sullivan!" Victoria shouts from the porch. "Come on out. Everyone's waiting."

"Let's go," Sullivan says, stuffing another brownie in his mouth. (Ick. To think I let that mouth kiss me yesterday.)

"You go alone, Sullivan. I'm serious. I don't look good."

This is absolutely true. I have flour and cornmeal in my hair, and god-only-knows-what dripped and splashed all over my shirt like a Jackson Pollock painting.

While a million imaginary red ants crawl around my rib cage, biting into my flesh, Sullivan chews his brownie and scrutinizes the multicolored blobs on my shirt. He laughs. "You look…scrumptious. Now, come on." He holds his hand out for me.

I whack it away. "No! I'm not going out there."

But it's no use. Sullivan's eyes twinkle like he just came up with a spectacular idea.

Oh no.

NONONONONONONO! I scream in my head. Except that Judy must have understood me, because she leaps to her feet, whimpering.

"Sullivan, I mean it!" I plead. "I—"

Sullivan lunges at me, laughing demonically. He grabs me around the waist, hoists me over his shoulder like a fifty-kilo bag of kibble and carries me kicking and screaming out the kitchen door, down the porch steps and out onto the field where everyone is assembled. They're all laughing as if they think Sullivan and I are having a gas, starring in some orchestrated stunt for everyone's amusement.

What happens next is all over in ten seconds, but it will play over and over in my nightmares for decades, I'm sure.

Maybe forever.

Somehow my thrashing legs knock over the photographer's tripod. He catches it mere seconds before his expensive camera crashes to the ground.

I puke down Sullivan's back, all the way to his red-and-white-striped high-tops. Picture it. I'd recently eaten my fill of leftover potato salad and sliced watermelon.

Sullivan drops me.

"I'm so-ho-ho-ho-ho so-ho-ho-ho sorry," he whispers, kneeling down to where I'm sprawled on the grass. Except he's not. He's laughing so hard he can barely talk.

"Fuck you, Sullivan!" I intend to scream, but only a garbled gasp escapes my mouth, punctuated by a final dribble of puke that slides off my chin onto the ground.

Around me, people are still laughing. The photographer has reassembled his camera and tripod. A powerful flash lights up the dusky field like a nuclear blast.

"Are you okay?" Sullivan asks. Suddenly, he's not laughing anymore.

I have no time to answer, because there's a loud crash in the kitchen, followed by Judy bursting through the screen door, one table leg dragging behind her. She races down the porch stairs, meeting the tripod and camera like a linebacker. The photographic equipment and the photographer go flying into the air. Judy gallops past the crowd at full speed down to the dock. Without a moment's hesitation or a backward glance, even when the table leg snags on a rock and the leash breaks, she bounds off the wharf and splashes into the St. Lawrence River.

TWENTY-TWO

I jump up and run after Judy, wiping hot tears of humiliation away with my hands so I can see where I'm going.
Already Judy is more than fifty feet from shore; at this
speed she'll be shaking herself off on the mainland in less
than twenty minutes. I race to the boathouse and toss a
paddle and a life vest into the canoe.

"Sarah! Wait!" Sullivan is at my heels. "Let's take the
motorboat."

I jump into the canoe and push off, picking up the
paddle, only barely resisting the urge to smash Sullivan
over the head with it.

"Sarah. Please." Sullivan kicks off his high-tops and
takes off his shirt, using it to hastily wipe puke off the back
of his shorts and legs.

"LEAVE ME ALONE!"

Sullivan dashes into the boathouse for a second paddle
and life vest. With a running start, ignoring Victoria's
shouts to stop right there, he jumps off the wharf and

into the bow of the canoe before I can work up enough momentum to drown him in my wake.

"Sarah, I'm sorry!" Sullivan calls to me over his shoulder. "Don't be mad! I'll make it up to you! I'll—"

"Just shut the hell up and paddle!" I yell at his bony back.

"I shouldn't have picked you up right after you'd eaten!"

"You shouldn't have picked me up at all!"

"Oh, come on! I was just having a bit of fun," he laughs. "I bet you didn't think a scrawny guy like me could carry you, did you?"

"I told you I didn't want to get my picture taken!"

"Nobody likes to get their picture taken—except maybe Johanna. But Dr. Fred needs publicity if he wants donations. And he needs donations to keep this place operating."

"I don't care!" Except that, as pissed off as I am, I do care. And now I've wrecked everything for Dr. Fred, after he was so nice to me today.

"Every time you go into a store or use a bank machine you're being photographed," Sullivan says.

"Don't remind me!"

"And someday you'll have your own cooking show on TV."

"THE HELL I WILL!"

Judy whips her head over her shoulder, sees the canoe gaining on her and figures out that she's being chased. Good. My arms are getting tired. Maybe she'll just lead us back to shore the way she does after her usual evening swim.

But instead she bolts ahead, hanging a left and starting upriver, toward Kingston and the Great Lakes. At this pace, she'll be docking in Chicago sometime next week.

Sullivan and I put our shouting match on hold for a moment to focus on our paddling, and we manage to maneuver around Judy. The goal is to get her turned back toward Moose Island. But Judy shoots to the right again.

"JUDY!" I call, reaching into the front pocket of my shorts for one of the several lint-covered dog biscuits I keep there, the canine equivalent of spare change. I hold the biscuit out over the side of the canoe as Sullivan tries to steer us up and around to block Judy's progress.

"Judy, come!" I repeat.

But Judy does not come. Judy shoots me another look, one of fear now, and tries to bolt again, but she doesn't seem to know where to go.

"JUDY!" I scream. "COME!"

But Judy just whimpers and starts to thrash around.

Then, oh my god, she begins to sink, her gigantic black head slipping farther below the dark river with each small wave. In seconds, her eyes go wild with fear. Then they close. They open again a second later, full of resignation. Her head slips under the water and stays under. She bobs there, motionless, just under the water.

Without a moment's hesitation, my heart pounding, my breath coming in a series of gasps, I kick off my sneakers, pull off the long T-shirt and denim shorts that will weigh me down, and dive out of the canoe into the river.

"Throw me a life jacket!" I yell up at Sullivan when I surface.

"Uh…Sarah, should you be—"

"NOW!"

Summoning every ounce of my upper-body strength, I push the jacket down under the water and pull Judy's front paws through the armholes. I am relieved to see the foam neck rest lift her head out of the water. I blow hard on her face, and the big dog rears back and coughs out what seems like a bucket of water. She begins thrashing again. A paw hits my face. Her nails scratch my cheek.

"Toss me the other jacket too!" I yell at Sullivan.

I push the second life jacket down under Judy's rear end until her hind legs are poking through the armholes and her butt is floating.

"Now throw me the rope!"

Sullivan unties the long rope from the front of the canoe and tosses it out to me. With Judy still floundering on top of the life jackets, I manage to tread water and fasten one end around her body like a crude harness.

Flipping onto my back, I tie the other end of the rope around my waist.

"Calm down. Relax. That's a good girl," I whisper to Judy, who slowly begins to melt into her life-jacket bed as if it's an air mattress.

Glancing around at my options, I decide not to back-stroke toward Camp Dog Gone Fun right away. There's a tiny island another hundred feet upriver, no more than two small pine trees poking up between three huge boulders.

Too small to support a doghouse, let alone a real house. But all I want is a landing spot to let Judy rest, so it'll do.

Arriving at dry land, Judy doesn't need coaxing to shed the life jackets and scramble up onto the rocks. She shakes about fifty gallons of river water out of her fur and then sits stoically atop the biggest of the three boulders, her tongue lolling out the side of her mouth, her chest heaving as she catches her breath.

A few minutes later, Sullivan pulls the canoe up alongside the rocks. I think about it a minute, deciding that even if we let her rest for an hour, I don't trust Judy to dog-paddle back to Camp Dog Gone Fun. The sun is down now, the sky will be black soon, and if she were to bolt again, the river would be too dark and dangerous to track her. And while the current is small potatoes this close to the mainland, if she were to panic and find her way out to the shipping lanes, there's no way two scrawny-armed teenagers in a canoe could do anything to help.

"Judy, get in the boat!" I command the big dog.

She balks.

I have no more patience. I only pulled the Judy-raft the length of two swimming pools, but my heart is pounding in my ears. Hands on my knees, I suck air into my lungs.

"JUDY! GET IN!" I scream. Grabbing the big dog by the scruff of her neck, I yell, "MOVE IT!" With me pushing and Sullivan pulling, and nearly capsizing twice, we manage to get all Judy's dog-bulk settled into the bottom of the canoe. "DOWN!" I tell her. With the rope we short-leash Judy to the middle thwart in case she gets any bright ideas about jumping out.

"Go ahead and sulk all you like," I tell her as she yawns and sets her head down on the bottom of the canoe, her forehead lowered and her mouth drooping in a frown.

Sullivan's jaw is down to his knees. "Man, can you swim! Sarah, where did you learn to—"

"Toss me my clothes!" I demand, my voice raspy from all the yelling. I can't believe I'm standing on a boulder in the middle of the St. Lawrence River in my wet underwear. Sure it's dusk, but there's still enough light to see that I might as well be naked.

Balancing on the slippery rock, I quickly pull my dry T-shirt and shorts over my wet underwear.

"This is all your fault," I mumble to Judy as I take my place in the canoe's stern.

No, I correct myself. It's Sullivan's fault.

Slowly and silently, I steer us back in the direction of Moose Island.

My mother would tell me that it's my own stupid fault. If I'd just gone out and had my damn picture taken, then—

It's my father's fault. As usual.

Isn't blaming your father for everything getting old, Sarah? the voice in my head whispers.

Shut the hell up, I think.

"Seriously, Sarah, where'd you learn to swim like that?" Sullivan asks, swiveling in his bow seat until he's facing me. He knows that Riverwood has no town pool. There's no swimming elective in gym class. I've never mentioned my family having a lake house—which we don't. Or admitted to spending previous summers at sleepaway camp—which I hadn't.

Good question, I tell myself. "Watching *Little Mermaid* videos?" I reply, gesturing for him to turn around and get paddling. Canoeing after dark is dangerous. Canoeing after dark when Victoria is your bow-paddler's mother could prove fatal.

But Sullivan can't take a hint. "Where did you take swimming lessons? I wanted to take—"

"I've never been swimming in my life."

"Yeah. Right."

"You know how lots of people joke around that they'd rather be dead than be seen in a bathing suit?"

"Sure."

"I'm the one who really means it."

"But out there? In the water? How did you know what to do?"

"I don't know. I was high on adrenaline. Haven't you heard stories about old ladies lifting cars off trapped kittens? Judy's okay. That's all that matters to me. Sullivan?"

"Yeah?"

I point my paddle over his shoulder. "Watch out for that piece of driftwood."

Lucky for us, the current is taking us back in the general direction of Moose Island without much effort. Which is good, because Sullivan is totally ADD when it comes to paddling.

"So, Sarah," he yaps, "if Mom doesn't kill me for ruining the party tonight, are we still—"

"You didn't ruin the party. I did."

"Nah. It was totally my fault. Mom's big on 'No Means No.' You definitely said no."

"That just refers to sex."

"Are you kidding? It refers to everything—except chores and basic hygiene, I guess. Anyway, are we still on for the puzzle and the concert? You aren't going to try to dump me again are you? I swear, I was just joking around tonight. I didn't know how strongly you felt about—"

I put my hand up, palm out. "Sullivan. It's okay. We're cool." I haven't got the strength to argue with him any more today.

"Thanks, Sarah!" He does a little happy dance in his seat; then he swivels around to resume paddling.

Sullivan is like Judy in some ways. Obnoxious at times, often infuriating, but too goofy and good-natured to stay mad at for long. Something about him makes me want to scratch his belly and ruffle his ears. Or the human equivalent anyway.

I look down at Judy. "We're cool too," I tell her, realizing it's true. "I'm glad you're okay."

Too tired to lift her head, she sticks out her neck and licks my big toe.

The mayor's boat is just pulling away as Sullivan and I approach the dock. The mayor laughs and waves to us from the deck of his cabin cruiser, like everything's just peachy.

Sullivan swings around in his seat again and raises an *Is this too good to be true?* eyebrow at me.

I shrug, distracted by the need to inspect the skin on my arms. No itching or explosive green pustules yet. Maybe the St. Lawrence isn't as polluted as everyone says.

"Go take a shower if you want," Sullivan says a few minutes later as we're hanging our life-jackets and paddles in the dark boathouse, doing our best to avoid Victoria.

"No time. I have to settle Judy in the barn and then finish scrubbing the chili pot. And I need to find the damn table leg. And figure out how to reattach it. No rest for the wicked, as my mom likes to say."

Sullivan nuzzles my river-slime-scented neck. "Don't worry about it. I'll do Judy and the pot."

"And the table?"

"My pleasure."

What's that saying? Never kiss a gift horse on the mouth? "Do a good job," I say, dashing into the night.

"Hey, Sarah!" Sullivan calls after me.

I turn.

"Joan of Arc was left-handed!"

I laugh. "So is Bart Simpson."

TWENTY-THREE

The next morning I'm in my cabin, changing out of my grease-spattered breakfast-cooking clothes, when someone comes knocking.

"Anyone home?" a singsong voice calls. Victoria. I'd slip out the back door if there was one.

"Hang on a second!" I shout, frantically pulling on my standard baggy shorts and T-shirt.

A few seconds later, I open the door and a red-faced, post-run Victoria pokes her head into the cabin, her forehead dripping sweat on the linoleum.

"Can I use your shower?" she asks. "The one in the lodge is backed up." Bundled in Victoria's arms are shampoo, conditioner, a towel and clean clothes.

I step out of the way, holding the door open so Victoria can enter, even though my first instinct is to push her out and wedge the door closed with a chair—except I don't have a chair. No locks. No chairs. No back doors.

No fun at all.

Without a moment's hesitation, Victoria begins stripping off her sweaty workout clothes.

I cringe at her lack of self-consciousness. "I'll just be...uh...going," I tell her, waving over my shoulder and opening the door just wide enough to dart through.

"Sarah, could you wait?" Victoria calls to me. "I'll only be a few minutes in the shower. I want to talk to you about something."

I don't think I can handle being reamed out about what happened last night. But then, I don't think Victoria cares much about my comfort zones. From the set of her jaw, I can tell she has what we here at Camp Dog Gone Fun call a bone to pick.

With me.

As promised, not three minutes later she bounds out of the shower stall and proceeds to dry herself off and pull on Lycra gym shorts, a matching tank top and hot pink flip-flops. With great agility, Victoria vaults herself up onto my loft bed as I continue to distract myself from her presence by rushing around the small space, dusting cobwebs from corners and shoveling my scattered laundry items into a basket. She tips her head up to read the graffiti previous "volunteers" have etched into the wooden rafters: *Kelli was here, July 2001. Darrell loves Paris Hilton! Mikalah sucks dogs.*

"You haven't written anything, Sarah," she comments.

"Nothing to say."

Victoria peers down at me, her forehead pleated like an accordion. "Dr. Fred and I have been talking about what happened yesterday during the mayor's visit."

The two pieces of toast I forced myself to eat that morning whip around in my stomach like they're on a Tilt-a-Whirl. I set the laundry basket down.

"Are you going to send me home?" I ask. Might as well cut to the chase.

If I'm expelled from Camp Dog Gone Fun, the judge might send me to youth detention for the rest of the summer. Despite what happened yesterday, here's the sorry truth: I don't want to leave. I can do without the cooking. And even the dog-biscuit contract, I guess. But I need Sullivan to get me to Ottawa. And Judy, that big hairy pain-in-the-ass, needs me. I lay awake all last night wondering what compelled her to torpedo into the river. And, maybe more importantly, wondering what compelled me to strip off my clothes and dive in after her when I thought my stripping days were over.

All I know is Judy better not try a stunt like that again.

Victoria jumps down off the bed. Landing softly on the balls of her feet, she reaches forward and grabs me by the shoulders. "Send you home? Don't be crazy, Sarah. Why would we want to send you home?"

Is this a trick question? "Because I ruined your picnic."

"You made our picnic wonderful, Sarah! All that delicious food! And Sullivan explained to me how quick-thinking you were out in the water with Judy. I'd say you saved the day!"

"But…the photographer. I…puked. I—"

"Sarah, that incident, whatever it was, wasn't your fault. I'm so ashamed that Sullivan—"

"Don't blame Sullivan," I sigh. "Please don't punish him. He was just trying to be…funny."

All I don't need right now is for Victoria to punish Sullivan by taking away his concert tickets.

She nods. "The mayor is putting a positive spin on the situation as well. His son spent a summer here a few years back too, if you catch my drift. Of course, he's disappointed about not getting his annual group shot for the paper, but thankfully the camera wasn't damaged when Judy knocked it off the tripod. As far as our visitors were concerned," Victoria continues, "you and Sullivan and Judy were just part of a hilarious prank. They even thought the vomit was some old-fashioned can-of-soup trick."

I'm halfway through a sigh of relief when Victoria snorts. "But, as we say here at Camp Dog Gone Fun, make no bones about it; I don't believe it for a second. You want to tell me what all that was about last night?"

The lightning in her eyes assures me that an emphatic NO! would be the wrong answer.

So I crack my knuckles, stare at the floor and speak the truth. "I just…I don't like…I can't…get my picture taken."

Victoria bursts out laughing. It's Sullivan's laugh, only two octaves higher. "Why? Are you a witch?" she cackles.

I know Victoria is just teasing, referring to one of Dr. Fred's demented campfire stories about how, in medieval times, left-handers were considered witches and were burned at the stake. During more modern times, he said, there persists a belief that witches can't be photographed.

Still, I'm tempted to ask Victoria where the hell she got her social worker degree. The back of a cereal box?

But I just shrug and tell her, "I wish," as I fantasize about flying out the window on a broomstick.

Victoria's face freezes mid-giggle. She stares at me like I've given her some great unexpected gift.

Damn, fuck, shit. I've said too much.

Victoria slumps down on the floor and rests her back against the cool drywall. She pats the floor beside her. "Let's sit." Not a suggestion, I realize, so I sit across from her, leaning against the bed frame.

Victoria takes a long breath. "I have to ask you something, Sarah." She pauses for what seems like a year. The flies in the overhead light fixture create a deafening buzz in my ears. "How much does this picture-taking issue of yours have to do with you being sentenced to Camp Dog Gone Fun this summer?"

I roll my eyes around, pretending not to understand the question.

Victoria persists. "I'll tell you why I asked, Sarah. See, I understand why the others ended up here, but you—"

"Doesn't my file say? I took my mother's boyfriend's car and—"

"Oh, I know what you did, Sarah. I just can't figure out why you did it."

Great. Here we are back at "Why, Sarah?" I thought I'd left all that behind in Riverwood.

"See, everyone else's why is easy to figure out…," Victoria adds, picking at her pink nail polish.

True enough. Taylor scratches her reasons in a notebook. Her Uncle Joe isn't just a perv; he's a devout Catholic perv and the father of the baby he paid Taylor two grand to abort. Nicholas steals junk food from corner stores because he has a compulsive eating disorder and his retired grandmother, with whom he lives, can't afford to give him the fat allowance he needs to feed it. Johanna's parents run a business that often takes them out of the country for weeks at a time. Bottom line: she has a big house, lots of friends and too much unsupervised time on her hands. Brant is just an asshole who can't resist a dare.

"...but you, Sarah," Victoria continues, "you've been here over a month. Your work is excellent. You have terrific rapport with the dogs. Your cooking is fabulous—congrats on the dog-biscuit contract, by the way. And Sullivan...adores you." She blushes. "My point is: I can't for the life of me figure out why you landed four hundred hours of community service."

Hey, God. How about a flash flood right about now?

"Do you need to know why?" I ask finally.

"No...but it might prevent a recurrence of—"

"Victoria, I've learned my lesson. I won't be stealing any more cars or driving like a maniac."

"But what—pardon the pun—drove you to do it in the first place?"

I stare straight ahead at a knot in the wood trim around the door frame, my elbows on my knees, my hands clenched under my chin.

"See," Victoria adds, "your impulsive actions last spring aren't the real issue, Sarah. They were just your response to an issue. And unless you deal with the issue, you may spend your life repeating—"

"I told you! I won't do it again!"

Victoria scootches across the room on her hands and butt until she is sitting next to me, her toes wiggling in her flip-flops. "I believe you, Sarah. But you might do something else just as—or more—destructive next time."

I wonder how much this interrogation has to do with Victoria wanting to help me and how much it has to do with her worrying that her precious Sullivan has a psycho girlfriend.

"Sarah, how much does having your photo taken— or not, as the case may be—have to do with why you are here?" Victoria prods.

I tilt my eyes up to the rafters and try to catch my breath. I can't do this.

Yes you can, the voice inside me says.

"Sarah?"

I snap my head up and glare at Victoria. She blinks in surprise, obviously never expecting to see such fire in my eyes. "Everything, okay! Everything!" My voice cracks. "Happy now?"

Victoria stays blessedly silent for a few seconds; then she says, "Sarah, I have to ask you something."

Hasn't she already asked enough?

"Are you being abused at home?"

"Nope." I track an ant crawling across the linoleum like it's the most fascinating thing on earth.

"Were you abused in the past?"

"Nope." I reach over my shoulder and scratch the back of my neck. Really dig my nails in. "Can I go now?" I ask, attempting to rise from the floor. "I need to exercise Judy before I can start lunch."

Victoria pulls me back down gently by the sleeve. "Just one more question."

I groan.

"Don't stress over it. I'm not asking as the camp social worker now. I'm asking as the mother of the guy who is gaga for you."

"Gaga?"

Victoria chuckles. "It's a compliment."

I bite my lips shut. If she starts lecturing me on birth control or something, I'm going to die. Kill myself. Sorry, Judy, you're on your own.

"Sullivan's birthday is in three days. Did he tell you?" Victoria asks.

I shake my head.

"Well…anyway…your cake for Trixie was such a hit. Would you make a cake for him too?"

I allow myself a small grin. "Does Sullivan want Eukanuba frosting too?"

Victoria considers this. "Maybe chocolate would be better."

"No problem." I try to rise again.

Again, Victoria puts her hand out to stop me. Victoria, who doesn't know when to shut up or, as we say here at Camp Dog Gone Fun, let sleeping dogs lie.

"You looked so relieved that all I asked for was a cake," she comments.

"No. It's just…"

"I know you think I'm probably too overprotective of Sullivan, and too strict—"

"Sullivan never said—"

"Oh, come on, sure he did. You know he was sick as a kid?"

I nod. "Leukemia. But he says he's cancer-free now, right?"

"But what he probably didn't tell you is that the chemo and other treatments blew out one of his kidneys and messed up his growth hormones so that he might always have what he calls Great Dane feet attached to a greyhound body. And"—Victoria sighs—"he has the liver function of a forty-year-old alcoholic."

"He has a good heart," I blurt out. He'd have to, to put up with me the way he does. And to put up with a mother who just spilled all his secrets. And for what? So I'd spill mine? Try again, Victoria.

Victoria takes a deep breath. Lets it out slowly. "So do you, Sarah," she replies, her eyes welling up.

Obviously, Victoria is no mind reader.

"Don't you see?" she continues. "Both of you are able to see beyond the surface warts to what matters most in each other."

For the record, I do not have warts.

Victoria jumps up into a standing position, reaches out a hand and pulls me up. She puts her hand on the cabin door, as if to leave, then turns back. "And Sarah? I suspect that whatever it is you're dealing with right now, it can't be easy."

Suspect all you like, Victoria. Try torturing the truth out of me. Won't work.

"You know what the best thing is about going through tough times?" she blathers on.

Haven't a clue.

"It's coming out the other side."

Just keep telling yourself that, Victoria. If she really believes that "tough times" don't trail you as doggedly as gas after a bean feast, why does she worry so much about Sullivan?

TWENTY-FOUR

The day before Sullivan's birthday, he leaves for town with Dr. Fred just after breakfast. He's meeting his dad for an early birthday visit and won't be back at Camp Dog Gone Fun until dinner the next evening.

Two hours later, Dr. Fred returns to Moose Island toting six grocery bags stuffed with all the ingredients I need to prepare Sullivan's birthday dinner. Victoria is paying, so the Camp Dog Gone Fun food budget took a backseat to the thirty-seven–ingredient lasagna I've been itching to make all summer. (My father used to charge twenty bucks a slice. It's that good.)

By midafternoon, after Judy duties and lunch duties and putting my huge lasagna into the fridge to set overnight, I go to work on the serious mother of all Black Forest cakes.

Judy and several of her three- and four-legged buddies are locked out on the porch, away from the dark chocolate, their wet noses pushed up against the door screen. Since I've started making a fresh batch of dog biscuits every morning,

I've become very popular with the canine crowd. They follow me around like I'm the Pied Piper of Moose Island.

When the cake is baked and cooled and iced and decorated, I hide it away in the back of the fridge behind a mountain of broccoli to protect it from Nicholas's prying fingers.

Now what? I wonder, slamming the fridge door and slipping out of the kitchen in search of Victoria. I need to discuss the birthday gift I've planned for Sullivan. It's a surprise that will absolutely demand that I stay up after—way after—lights-out tonight.

I find her filing paperwork in Dr. Fred's office and quickly tell her what I'm planning.

"Well, I bet he'll like that a lot better than what I got him," she laughs, opening a desk drawer and pulling out a bulky, wilted-celery-green sweater. "It's organic wool," she says, like that makes it all better. "Good for back-to-school, don't you think?"

Ick.

"So I can break curfew tonight?" I ask.

Victoria reaches out and squeezes my arm. "Stay up as long as you need to."

TWENTY-FIVE

Midmorning on Sullivan's birthday, Tiara, a fourteen-year-old boxer, curls up in the breezy shade beside the boathouse for her usual morning nap.

And dies there a half hour later, peaceful and content.

Dr. Fred puts on a tie, gathers everyone together on the dock and reads a few short stories from *Chicken Soup for the Dog Lover's Soul*. Then he wraps the old girl up in a flannel blanket and sets out in the motorboat to the mainland, to his clinic, to do whatever needs to be done. Nobody asks what that is, and Dr. Fred doesn't say. Moose Island is too rocky to bury a rawhide, let alone a dog. Stupid Brant would make *Pet Semetary* jokes anyway. Tiara deserves better.

My dog, Brownie, never had a funeral. My mother and I took him to the vet in Riverwood to be put down the day he became too weak to eat. Leaving the clinic clutching Brownie's smelly leather collar in my fist, I felt only a heavy, heavy sadness and a ton of guilt. Brownie had been the best dog he knew how to be. It wasn't his fault he had been dragged into the drama of my life. But just as fiercely as I'd loved him, I'd also resented having to protect him from my father. Or had it really been my *father* I was protecting? Why? Did the part of me that loved my father hold out faint hope that one day he'd stop taking photographs of me? That my mother would take her head out of her latest novel? That we could be a normal family?

Sullivan arrives back at Camp Dog Gone Fun just in time for his birthday dinner, wearing a new pair of high-tops—black with yellow happy faces.

The lasagna and the Black Forest cake are wild successes. Even skinny Johanna ends up wearing smudges of tomato sauce and chocolate-cream filling on her face.

Victoria gives Sullivan her gift—the ugly sweater. Sullivan, being the good son that he is, tries not to gag. "That's…nice, Mom. Very…practical."

Dr. Fred reaches into his back pocket and pulls out a one-hundred-dollar Future Shop gift certificate.

"Hey! Thanks!" Sullivan exclaims.

"Maybe you should stock up on back-to-school supplies," Victoria suggests.

"Maybe you should pick out some music and DVDs," Dr. Fred says, winking as Sullivan reaches across the table to give his hand a boisterous shake.

Nicholas passes over a homemade greeting card from all the "volunteers" that he made with scraps of craft materials he scrounged up in the rec room. Taylor took a break from writing her usual dark poetry to pen a jaunty birthday limerick inside.

Johanna bats her eyelashes at Sullivan and generously offers to give him what she calls a *man*-icure, which Sullivan politely declines.

Brant slugs him on the shoulder, reaches into his back pocket and pulls out a strip of multicolored condoms. "Go crazy, kid," he adds, tossing them into Sullivan's lap as Victoria chokes on her Diet Coke. Slowly, I start to slide under the table. Sullivan's face turns red as the sunset as the others hoot with laughter.

"Well...," Dr. Fred says, glancing at his watch. "I guess it's time to see to the dogs."

"No...wait. I have something for Sullivan too," I pipe up.

"I'll just bet you do!" Nicholas guffaws, leering at the condoms Sullivan has removed from his lap and set on the table beside his can of 7-Up.

"Fuck off, Nicky!" I explode.

"Five bucks, Sarah," Victoria responds wearily.

"Nicholas should pay the fine," Taylor says, taking my side. "He's the one who can never keep his fat trap shut. And you're a jerk!" she says, turning to Brant and pounding him on the arm.

"You know what they say about guys with big feet, don't you, Sarah?" Johanna giggles.

"You know what they say about girls with big mouths?" Victoria says sharply.

I clear my throat. "Uh…anyway, Sullivan. Your gift is in the storage shed."

"Maybe you should go and get it, Sullivan," Victoria suggests. "Sarah and I'll clean up the kitchen. Dr. Fred and the others can head to the barn."

Sullivan sure looks like he could use some fresh air.

I wash the dishes while Victoria wipes crumbs off the table and arranges Sullivan's gifts—even the condoms—into a neat pile for him to take up to his room later.

Tension hangs in the air like the smell of boiled cabbage. "Victoria…," I say, "about the…you don't need to worry…we're not…"

"Not yet," she sighs.

Not ever. Not once Sullivan finds out I'm just using him to get into the city next weekend.

Come on, Sarah. That annoying voice in my head asserts itself again. *You know you like him.*

Doesn't matter, I argue. I have to find the photos and destroy them. Nothing else matters. Not even Sullivan's friendship.

Not just his friendship, Sarah. It's more than that.

I don't care! I have to find the pictures. Sullivan's just a means to an end.

You don't believe that for a minute.

"You okay?" Victoria asks from across the room. She's been studying my face. Trying to discover my secrets in the set of my jaw and the way I wrinkle my nose and push loose strands of hair out of my eyes.

"Uh...sure." I turn my attention back to the dishes.

Sullivan bursts through the screen door and wraps his arms around me, giving me a rib-cracking squeeze and swinging me around the kitchen. Soap bubbles fly everywhere as I fight him off with the yellow rubber gloves.

"You finished the puzzle!" He lets me go and turns to his mother. "Mom! Did you see it? I'm free!"

Victoria nods. "I have a bit of a surprise too, Sullivan. You can take the boat over to the mainland as soon as Sarah has exercised Judy and settled her down for the night. That new Bond movie you've been raving about opens tonight. I thought you two might like to see the early show."

Sullivan does another little celebratory dance around the kitchen table.

"I checked the movie times," Victoria continues. "So I expect you back by ten thirty. And remember your cell phone, Sullivan. And to test the boat lights before you go; it will be dark when you start back."

"We're traveling half a mile over to Gananoque, not heading overseas on the *Titanic*," Sullivan laughs.

"That reminds me," Victoria adds. "Remember your life-jackets. And the oars in case the motor gives you trouble. *And* the bail bucket. And for heaven's sake, find a safe place to tie up, Sullivan."

He nudges me. "Ain't freedom grand?"

"Don't be a smart-mouth," Victoria says, pulling her son into a hug. "I can't believe my baby's seventeen." She pulls away, muttering, "I can't believe my baby got condoms for his birthday."

Sullivan grins. "What's that you always say, Mom? 'Better safe than sorry.'"

"That's what I say to other kids, not my kid..." Victoria groans. "Who knew how soon those words would come back and bite me on the..."

Say it, Victoria. Say ASS. I dare you. *A-S-S*, I think.

"...you know where."

Sullivan holds my hand through the movie. After one particularly ghastly explosion, he leans over. "I'm surprised Mom didn't force us to see the new Disney movie playing next door instead," he whispers. His breath smells like lasagna and Skittles.

I wish Victoria had. I'm relieved when, minutes later, Sullivan's eyes stay riveted to the screen during a skanky topless scene. That way, he doesn't notice me clenching mine shut.

We arrive back at Moose Island at 10:32 PM.

"Don't worry. Mom has a five-minute grace period." Sullivan runs into the lodge to let Victoria know we are back. And to tell her he's walking me to my cabin.

"Did she check your pockets?" I ask when he returns.

"For what?"

"For the condoms. Do you have them with you?"

"Shit...I could go back...," Sullivan whispers.

I laugh. "I'm joking. And that'll be five bucks for the cuss fund." I hold out my hand.

Sullivan drapes an arm around my shoulder and steers me toward my cabin. "*Shit's* only a buck fifty."

"Aren't you the bargain hunter."

If this were a scene in one of my chick-lit novels, I'd focus on the moonlight reflecting off the spikes of Sullivan's hair. The huskiness in his voice. The warmth of his hand on my shoulder.

But this isn't a novel. This story won't end happily ever after. Sullivan and I are doomed.

If you insist, the annoying voice inside me replies.

It's true, damn you.

Then maybe, the voice persists, *you should just enjoy this night while it lasts.*

TWENTY-SIX

Fifteen minutes later, Sullivan and I are making out in my loft bed, counting off the minutes until 11:00 PM, when Dr. Fred bursts in.

"Sarah!" he gasps, completely ignoring Sullivan, or perhaps not even seeing him in the dark. "You have to get up! Your mother just arrived! The police and your lawyer are here too!"

Dr. Fred tries the light switch.

"It's burned out," I say, my thoughts screaming SHITSHITSHITSHIT—at least fifty dollars worth.

The light's not burned out. When I wouldn't let him get his hand under my shirt because the light was shining on me like a spotlight, Sullivan, in a show-off move that would have horrified his mother, shimmied across the rafters from my bed and loosened the bulb.

"It never crossed your mind to just lean over me and pull the cord?" I asked him when he shimmied back and wasted three minutes of good make-out time picking a splinter out of his palm.

"Nah. Too easy. It'll be better when we get back to Riverwood. The light in my bedroom at Dad's house has a clapper," Sullivan said, like he really thinks we'll still be making a go of it in September.

Now Dr. Fred holds the cabin door open and frantically gestures for me to hurry. But I feel paralyzed. Trapped in a nightmare. I can't see Sullivan's face in the dark, but I can feel the confusion in his eyes. The curiosity. The caring. It's piercing my skin. Making me ache. Because there's only one reason why my mother and a cop and my lawyer would trek out to Moose Island in the middle of the night.

Only one.

Mom has found the Hush Puppies box. She's seen the Polaroids.

"Sarah!" Dr. Fred's voice is sharp now. "I don't know what this is about, but your mom seems very upset. She's with Victoria at the lodge."

I can't breathe. I lumber down from the loft bed, stumbling when I reach the floor. My knees will barely support my weight. I grab the bedpost with one hand to keep from tumbling to the floor and somehow find the sense to use the other to straighten my twisted-up shirt.

Dr. Fred speaks more softly. "Sullivan, I know you're up there too. Come with me, son. Let's check on the dogs."

When I slink up the porch stairs and through the screen door into the kitchen, Mom starts to stand up but then slides wordlessly back into her chair.

Slumped at the kitchen table, she sports a frozen grimace that I imagine is equal parts shock and horror about the situation and disgust and anger with me. Her skin, spotlit under the too-bright kitchen bulb, is a sickly pale green, like she's been throwing up all evening. Her eyes are red-rimmed and dry, like she's cried for hours even after her tears have run dry. She can't stop blinking, even though each rapid lash movement makes her wince. I haven't seen such a stunned and horrified expression on anyone—at least not since seeing the TV images of people in New York on 9/11.

The old cardboard Hush Puppies box has been duct-taped shut. It sits in the middle of the kitchen table like a cheesy centerpiece.

Does she want to hug me? Slap me? Disown me? Nothing would surprise me now. Mom didn't even look this bad when she found out Dad had choked to death.

My heart is a jackhammer. I'm sure the thumps are audible—maybe even visible—right through my thick sweatshirt. I haven't taken a full breath since Dr. Fred burst into my cabin, but oddly, I feel relieved.

Across the table, it seems as if the wheels in my mother's head have spun out, hit black ice. I imagine Mom struggling to understand how our little family suddenly turned into something so ugly, something that only happens in sad novels or to other people's families. I imagine her asking herself if we haven't already suffered enough, what with a dead husband/father and this community service business? I imagine her thinking about all the times she's chastised me about not wanting to get my picture taken, and finally figuring out where I was going—and why—the night I stole Tanner's car.

"You know what's in that box, don't you, Sarah?" My mother speaks, finally, her voice a raw croak. I nod slowly, dropping into the chair across from her, my eyes scanning the scene around us, grateful that my mother is at least smart enough to know not to touch me right now, or ask me if I'm okay.

Victoria is trying to be inconspicuous. But I can tell by the too-quiet way she is shuffling around at the sink in a bathrobe and pink fuzzy slippers, making coffee, that she is listening to every single word, every change of tone, between my mother and me. Her peripheral vision is taking in and analyzing every movement and posture.

And worse, she doesn't even seem shocked.

In a huddle across the room, the cop and my lawyer are grunting in low monosyllables, probably wishing they were home with their own less screwed-up families.

One bonus: Dr. Fred and Sullivan are taking an inordinately long time in the barn. Dr. Fred probably has an "all clear" signal worked out with Victoria. By the looks of things so far, it might be a long time coming. He and Sullivan might be better off bedding down with the dogs.

I think about staying up past four this morning, finishing Sullivan's stupid jigsaw, supposedly for his birthday but really for myself, to guarantee it would be done before the Ratgut concert.

All for nothing now.

"Why didn't you tell me what was happening to you?" Mom asks. "Christ, Sarah, I can tell by the pictures that this…horrific…business…was going on for years. We could have fired David! Sent him to jail! We still can. I—"

"NO! It wasn't—"

Mom sighs. "Sarah, I know these pictures were taken at the restaurant. I recognize the furniture in the back room. There's a team of police officers out looking for David now. I—"

"IT WASN'T DAVID! Please…" I swivel in my chair to address the cop. "Listen to me! Don't arrest David! It wasn't—"

"Sarah, what do you mean, it wasn't David?" The green drains from Mom's face, leaving it a ghostly gray. She speaks softly, slowly now. "He and your father were the only ones with access to—"

Clearly Mom isn't any better at puzzles than Sullivan. She can't piece this situation together even with all the ugly pictures right in front of her. Maybe because she doesn't want to.

I help her along. "It was Dad."

"Sarah, don't lie. Don't you dare tell me that. Your father would never do such a thing. He loved you, Sarah. He—"

"LISTEN TO ME! He said he'd kill Brownie if I ever told!"

My mother rises on shaky legs and reaches her arms out to me, but I stand and take a step back. I don't want a hug. It's too little, too late.

Victoria guides Mom back into her chair. Sliding the Hush Puppies box aside, she places a steaming cup of coffee on a place mat. Mom mumbles her thanks and eyeballs the coffee blankly, but I can see that her hands are shaking too much to take a sip without sloshing it everywhere.

The cop and my lawyer motion for me to follow them through the kitchen to the rec room. Someone has left a half-done Scrabble game on the coffee table. Little square letters are scattered everywhere. I imagine them sliding together to spell D-O-O-M-S-D-A-Y.

My lawyer, Barry Hendon, pulls the plaid armchair over to the couch and gestures for our small group to sit. "First of all, Sarah," he tells me, "I haven't looked at the pictures."

The cop has looked though. I can tell. He clears his throat too many times in a row and won't look me in the eye. In books, on TV shows and maybe even in big cities, they have sensitive, specially trained female cops and well-meaning social workers working round the clock to deal with cases like mine. Welcome to small-town reality, Sarah, I think. Despite my baggy clothes, I feel naked. Raw. Like a plucked chicken ready for the deep fryer.

Finally the cop leans forward and rakes his hands through the gray fringe of hair between his bald spot and his ears. "I know this is difficult, but I have to ask a few questions, Sarah. Your mother and Barry have given their permission to proceed. These questions will be uncomfortable for you, but I need to make sure that charges are laid where necessary."

"How can you charge a dead man?" I scoff.

He ignores my comment and flips open a notepad. He pulls a pen from his shirt pocket. "Now...you realize that what happened to you was a crime?"

I nod.

"I need a yes or no."

"Yes."

"Did anyone besides David Murray ever take pictures of you?"

"No! I told you! David didn't do anything! It only happened after David finished his shifts. Please don't tell David."

Once, when I was nine years old, David brought me a whole carton of old dog-eared Archie comics he'd collected as a kid, just because he knew I liked cartoons. He never expected, and never got, anything in return but my happy "Thanks, David!" I loved David like a big brother.

The lawyer cleared his throat. "Sarah, just answer the questions."

"But—"

"Where were the pictures taken?" the cop asked.

"In the storeroom. At my father's restaurant. By my *father*."

"Was anyone else ever in the room with you while the pictures were taken?"

"No. How many times do I—"

"Okay, okay. Did your *father,* to your knowledge, ever sell or give the pictures to anyone, or scan them onto the Internet?"

I gulp for air. "I don't think so."

"To your knowledge, did your *father* ever take pictures of anyone other than you?"

"I don't think so."

The cop sighs deeply and turns another page of his notebook. "Was your mother aware of what was happening?"

"I don't think so."

"You don't *think* so?"

"No. No, she wasn't."

"You never tried to tell her? Or any other adult?"

"No."

The cop raises both eyebrows. "And since your father's death, have you unwillingly—or willingly—participated in other—"

"NO! We're finished here." I push myself up from the couch. I took the law elective last semester. I know he can't force me to answer his questions. I wouldn't have answered *any* questions if they hadn't brought David into the equation. Just one more fucking person I need to protect. Why does no one ever protect me?

"Sorry," the cop says sheepishly, flipping his notebook closed and rising too. "That'll be all for now." I watch him stride back through the kitchen and out the screen door. In the orange glow of the porch light, I see him plunk his butt on the top porch step, light a cigarette and pull his cell phone out of his back pocket. I can't hear him talking over my mother's sobs, but I'd like to hope he's on the phone to whichever of his coworkers he's sent after David. I'd like to think that maybe this isn't just another day on the job for him. Just another day of busting up underage pit parties and chasing shoplifters. Maybe he hates what he had to do tonight, dredging up all my personal business.

Barry Hendon beckons me to sit back down. "I spoke to the judge, Sarah."

I groan and pound a fist on my knee. "How many people are going to know about this before it's over?"

"The courts will not release your name to anyone. Besides, if what you say can be backed up with evidence that your father owned a Polaroid camera…"

"He did. Ask my mom. He used the same camera for taking vacation photos. I don't know if we still have it. Dad used to keep the camera hidden from me too—probably so I wouldn't break it or steal it—but Mom might know where it is. And check his old credit card statements. There must be receipts for Polaroid film. Boxes and boxes of it."

"In that case, this situation probably won't even make the papers."

"But Riverwood is a small town. People talk." Except for Sullivan, who will probably never speak to me again once he finds out.

Barry glances at his watch. "Judge Mather checked through the statements given to police the night of your automobile incident last March and said that in light of these circumstances, your reaction to being photographed by your mother's boyfriend was understandable. Still inappropriate, but understandable. That said, you're free to go, Sarah. Tonight if you want to. I've got a couple of community service kids who might jump at the chance to replace you. Your outstanding community service hours will be erased. Take some personal time for the rest of the summer."

I cross my arms defiantly. "I'm not leaving."

"But...you don't have to stay anymore."

"I want to stay."

"You need time to..." He pauses, searching for a politically correct word. "Heal."

"I'm staying."

"But..." Barry Hendon stops, shrugs, snaps open his briefcase. He extracts his own cell phone and punches in what I assume is the judge's home number. "Kids," he mutters.

TWENTY-SEVEN

Ten minutes later the cop and the lawyer are eager to get back to the mainland. And since it's clear that I won't go with them—at least not without some sort of physical intervention—my mother begs them to wait. She can't just leave without talking to her daughter, can she?

To be honest, I wish she would.

"Couldn't all this have waited until the morning?" I ask her. We're standing at the head of the dock, while the cop and lawyer are at the foot, making more calls on their cell phones and preparing their boat for the short trip back to the mainland.

"I panicked, Sarah. When Tanner showed me the—"

"Tanner? Tanner found them?" I hiss, afraid of raising my voice and having someone overhear. "What the hell was Tanner doing at the restaurant? And come to think of it, what the hell were you doing at the restaurant? You promised me that you'd wait for me to—"

Mom sniffles. "I didn't break my promise about letting

you do inventory. It's just…the library is having a rummage sale next week. To raise funds for renovations to the children's wing. I thought it would be a nice idea to donate a few of your father's older cookbooks. Just a few, because I thought you'd want most of—"

"I don't want any of them."

"But…I thought you were all fired up to do the inventory. I thought—"

"I WANTED TO FIND THE PICTURES!"

Mom pulls a soggy tissue from her purse and blows her nose. "Tanner came with me to help carry books to the car. We were in the back room. I was pulling some dusty old spice encyclopedias off the bookshelf and found the shoe box lodged behind them. I passed the box to Tanner and asked him to check if the recipe cards inside were hand-written or typed. I thought if they were typed, we could bundle them up and sell them by lot."

Bile fills my throat. I picture Tanner's face as he opened the box and discovered stacks of kiddie porn. Tanner's bewilderment when he realized the subject of said kiddie porn was his girlfriend's daughter. The disgust that must have pierced his heart when he wondered if Mom knew about, or had a hand in, the abuse. The understanding that I had a damn fine reason for not wanting his camera pointed at my face that foggy night last March.

"Tanner told me I had to call the police right away. It just never, never, never—"

"Never. I get it," I mumble.

"—occurred to me that your father was behind this.

Are you absolutely sure it was Ian, Sarah? Maybe you were too upset to remember clearly. Maybe David—"

"DAVID NEVER DID ANYTHING TO ME!" I stomp my foot on the dock. "Face the fucking truth, Mom," I hiss. "You were married to a monster."

Mom buries her face in her shaking hands. "Sarah, I'm so, so sorry," she sobs. "Where the hell was I when all this was happening?"

"At the library," I tell her, whacking a mosquito on my left temple so hard that my ears ring. "With your nose in a book."

My mother makes a sound like a cat with its paw stuck in a mousetrap and tries to lay a hand on my shoulder.

I wrench myself away. "You're a librarian. It's your job. Don't sweat it, Mom."

It was like I'd hauled off and punched my mother in the face. She starts hyperventilating. "I just…I don't know how…I could have missed all this…going on."

"You worked Tuesday and Thursday nights. You still work Tuesday and Thursday nights."

Mom seems to have aged ten years in the past hour. Her face is wrinkled and flushed and defeated, like a half-deflated red balloon. "You mean…all those times I dropped you off…at the restaurant? Every time…?"

"Pretty much."

Mom turns away from me, hugging her arms around herself like a do-it-yourself straitjacket. She stares out over the dark water of the St. Lawrence. "Christ, Sarah," she mumbles, sucking in a long breath of damp night air and letting it out slowly. "All those times you wanted me to sign you up for Tuesday evening Girl Guides and Thursday night soccer and I said no, because Tuesday and Thursday were slow nights at the restaurant. Your father wanted to spend time with you. I thought he was being a good father, an involved father. He said he was going to teach you to cook when you were old enough."

"He did that too."

"Why didn't you at least tell me after he died? He couldn't have hurt Brownie then."

I take a deep breath and exhale slowly. "It was over then. All I wanted was to find the pictures and destroy them."

"But—"

"I told you! I didn't want you to know!" I hiss again. "I didn't want anyone to know. I still don't."

"But…why not? I'm your mother."

I shake my head at her stupidity. "I was trying to protect you. And to protect myself from being humiliated for one more second. But look at what's happened! You're freaking out! And the police and my lawyer and Victoria and Tanner and the judge and God-knows-who-else all know about it."

"Sarah, I—"

"Don't you see? As long as the pictures were my secret—something only I knew about—I thought I could fix things. Now, everything is just like you said—a mess."

Mom grabs my shirtsleeve and gives it a pull. "Come home with me, Sarah. Please. "

"No." I yank my arm back. "I'm staying. I can't go back to Riverwood right now. The dogs need me."

"I need you, Sarah."

"You have Tanner." He started this mess tonight; let him deal with my mother. I can't imagine how she feels, but if she feels even half as bad as she looks, she needs more than I can possibly give her right now.

"I can't face Tanner—or anyone else—right now," I tell her. "And I want the pictures," I demand, pointing to the Hush Puppies box that rests on the dock next to Barry Hendon's briefcase. Such an innocent-looking box with such explosive contents. "I want them tonight. Now. Don't let the police keep them."

Down at the dock, the cop and lawyer are trying to be polite and give me and my mother whatever time we need, but it is clear from the way they keep glancing at us and their watches, and pacing around impatiently, that they won't wait much longer. Mom looks trapped between wanting to stay with me and wanting to escape this madness. Between wanting to reach out to me and being afraid that I'll push her away.

I make it easy for her. "You have to go, Mom. Go home. Get some rest. Just leave the pictures."

"Sarah, I—"

"I want to burn them. I don't want anyone else to see them—ever!"

The cop and my lawyer start to saunter back up the dock, leaving the Hush Puppies box behind. The cop stops to light a cigarette.

I'm not a moron. I rush down the dock, grab the untended box and charge back at breakneck speed, elbowing past the cop, my lawyer and my mother. I run away from the dock, away from the lodge, all the way to my cabin, with the hated Hush Puppies box tucked under my arm like a football.

"Sarah!" Mom shouts after me.

"GO HOME, MOM! PLEASE!"

Over my shoulder, I flash her a peace sign.

No one comes after me.

TWENTY-EIGHT

I have a lighter in my knapsack. I've never smoked, but I stole the pink plastic Bic from the restaurant as soon as I was old enough to figure out how to use it. I always figured that if I was ever lucky enough to stumble across the photographs by accident, it would make sense to burn them before my father could stop me. If it meant burning the house or the restaurant to the ground in the process, so be it.

When I reach my cabin door, breathless from my sprint, I am shocked to find Judy tied to the railing of the steps. I'd bedded her down myself before leaving for the movies with Sullivan. But here she is, fast asleep, with a note tucked under her collar. It reads, in big awkward guy-printing:

Sarah, I don't know what's happening. Please let me know what I can do to help.
Sullivan. XOXOXOXOX

I can't deal with Sullivan right now.

I snatch the lighter from my pack, and with the Hush Puppies box still clutched under my arm, I rouse Judy and lead her by flashlight along the path to the beach.

There's a stiff breeze on this side of the island. Overhead, the sky is gloomy. I fear rain. I'll have to work fast. From the other side of the island, I hear a motorboat pulling away. Bye, Mom.

My thoughts turn to one of Dr. Fred's earlier bonfire chats. One about wilderness survival. More specifically, fire building.

Make a teepee, I remember. Dried leaves go on the bottom, then twigs, then sticks, then logs—in that order. Flick on the lighter. Touch it to the tinder. And…*WHOOSH!*

My fire is…spectacular.

I frantically rip the tape from around the Hush Puppies box. I toss pictures in the flames one at a time, upside down so I don't have to see the images, the puzzle pieces of my childhood, as they bubble and shrivel and peel before turning to ash.

A foul chemical stench pollutes the air.

Judy is lying upwind, out of the smoke, quiet but watchful. She may not understand my particular circumstances, but I want to believe she recognizes my emotions. In any case, it seems she knows that what I am doing is very, very important, and that it's not time for horseplay or interruptions or midnight swims.

Almost an hour later, when the last of the photographs are burned, I rip the Hush Puppies box into pieces and throw the chunks into the fire, where they sizzle and spit before succumbing to the flames. As much as I like dogs, I'll be happy if I never have to look at another basset hound as long as I live.

I lie back on the beach and stare up at the smoke-filled sky, oblivious to the pebbles and Judy's discarded fetch sticks poking into my back.

The big dog shuffles across the sand and rests her head on my lap. I place one of my hands on Judy's shaggy chest and feel her heart go *kaboom, kaboom, kaboom.* With my other hand, I rub her ears and let the breeze blow the ashes of my father's sins into the river, where they will travel past Montreal and Quebec City to the Atlantic. But my memories of the terror and humiliation refuse to budge.

TWENTY-NINE

I straggle from my cabin to the flagpole the next morning, Judy tugging me merrily along after another sleepover. Since I don't need to draw straws for duties—I only need to prove I'm awake and mobile—I walk wordlessly past the flagpole, past the barn, past the stares, and down to the dock, where I spend my usual first half hour of the morning tossing sticks for Judy and deciding what to make for breakfast.

"Hey," Sullivan says, sidling up beside me and bumping his hip against mine. His spiky hair is flattened on one side and he smells like guy-sweat and flannel and dog, like maybe he really did sleep in the barn last night.

"Hey, yourself."

"I've got ten minutes before I need to start scooping out the kibble. You okay?"

"Sure," I reply, throwing a stick into the water for Judy, who takes after it like a missile. The big dog's bizarre near drowning less than a week ago seems to have had no lasting effect on her love of the water. I'd still like to know what made her flip out that night of the Dog Daze Festival. Unfortunately, I've been too flipped out myself to give it much serious thought. Dr. Fred's explanation is that dogs are just like that sometimes when they get overexcited. Some barf. Some bite. And some bolt.

Just like humans.

"Is everything okay with your mom?" Sullivan asks.

"I guess."

"You aren't leaving Moose Island, are you?"

"Nope."

"Are you in trouble?"

"Not really."

"Am *I* in trouble?"

I turn and gape at Sullivan. His blue eyes are so… clueless. "Huh?"

"Well…I thought maybe your mom called for you when we were in town last night. Maybe freaked when you weren't here? I don't know…maybe you aren't allowed to date yet? Or maybe she thinks you're only here to work?"

"You really don't know what happened last night?"

Sullivan shakes his head. "Mom won't even tell Dr. Fred what happened last night. She says we don't need to know unless you want us to."

Yay, Victoria.

I reach out and squeeze Sullivan's hand. It's sticky with who-knows-what, but I don't care. "It's better this way. Trust me."

"Okay." Sullivan squeezes back, but I can tell he's confused and hurt that I'm not sharing. "Sarah?"

"Yeah?"

"If you change your mind, don't forget, you can trust me too."

Taylor is in the kitchen when I get there, slapping boxes of Raisin Bran and Corn Flakes onto the kitchen table. A punch bowl full of canned fruit cocktail is already there, a ladle plunked down next to it. The nauseating smells of burnt toast and way-too-strong coffee fight for airspace.

"Get the milk, would you," she orders me.

I am speechless. Immobile. Who the hell gave my job to Taylor?

"Just thought I'd help," she tells me. "Got a problem with that?"

"Uh...no...," I say. "I guess not." I've had less than four hours' sleep in the past forty-eight hours and don't have the energy to do more than scrape charcoal spots off the toast anyway.

"I never told anyone either," Taylor says a few minutes later as she "helps" me dump a heaping plate of toast and a jumble of jam and peanut butter jars on the table.

"Told anyone what?"

"Don't play dumb," she says, wiping her hands on a damp dish towel. "About what happened to me. The abuse. Not even after I got pregnant and had the abortion. I told everyone, even my mom, that the kid's father was some guy I met at a party one weekend."

I cock my head at her. "But...your poetry? About... Uncle Joe?"

"I never wrote a poem in my life until the morning I got here. Victoria told me I needed an 'outlet'—besides spray-painting churches and cutting myself."

"But...you seem so...comfortable...reading it out loud."

Taylor gapes at me. "Comfortable? It nearly kills me! But what's that saying? 'What doesn't kill you makes you stronger.' I'm not just here to shovel dog shit this summer. I'm here to toughen up. My plan requires it."

"Your plan?"

Taylor twirls her eyebrow ring around and around a few seconds. Then she clomps over to the kitchen door, peering out to make sure that we're alone. "My mom's birthday is coming up in a few weeks," she tells me. "I'm going to mail my poems to her, wrapped in pretty paper. Then she'll know all about what she could have prevented if she'd just opened her"—Taylor glances left and right, double-checking for signs of Victoria—"fucking eyes. I mean, the signs were everywhere."

Taylor pulls out a kitchen chair and plunks down at the table. "My final poem will be sweet and simple: 'Roses like sun. Violets like rain. Don't fucking expect to see me again.'"

"It makes a clear point," I tell her.

"When I leave Camp Dog Gone Fun, I'm hopping a Greyhound—the bus, not the dog—to Montreal. I got accepted with a full scholarship, including residence, at McGill. Don't look so damned surprised, Sarah. My body's been fucked over, but my mind's as sharp as that fancy knife you use."

Taylor pauses a minute, then asks, "So what did your mom find that brought her out here so fast last night? Videos? A journal? Or did your Uncle Joe get drunk and bring her the goods himself?"

"I don't have an Uncle Joe."

Taylor laughs. "You are so naïve. Neither do I. 'Uncle Joe' is my dad, the kind, upstanding, Catholic choirmaster who raped me."

"My father wasn't a rapist," I say quietly.

"Okay, so be in denial." Taylor crosses her arms over her chest.

"He never touched me!" I insist. "Ever."

Taylor scrapes her chair back. "You are so full of shit!" she hisses as she stalks off toward the rec room.

"Taylor, wait!" I call.

She steps back into the kitchen and stands awkwardly against the door frame, her hair as short and as green as a fresh-cut lawn, her chains and face jewelry and spiked neck and wrist collars as forbidding as a barbed wire fence.

"My father took photos," I tell her, gripping the counter for balance. "Polaroids. At his restaurant. After it closed every Tuesday and Thursday night. It started before I can even remember. When I got old enough to be uncooperative, he got me a dog and told me he'd run Brownie over with his car if I refused him or told my mother or anyone else."

I suck in a breath and hold it as long as I can before letting it out. "When he died a little over a year ago—"

"Lucky you," Taylor interjects.

"—the restaurant was boarded up while the legal and insurance stuff was sorted out. I figured I just had to make a copy of my mother's key, get into the city on my own, figure out where he hid the pictures and destroy them. Easy as pie."

"But, as we say here at Camp Dog Gone Fun, it's a dog-eat-dog world," Taylor says, laughing darkly. "You ended up here instead."

With shaking hands, I pour myself a coffee and take a huge gulp, burning my mouth. Sputtering, I continue. "My mother's boyfriend won a camera in a raffle at work. He was just joking around, wanting to try out his new camera on me."

Taylor yanks a chair out from the table again. I think she might be gearing up to pitch it across the room, but she just kicks it around and straddles it. "The sick bastard!" she says.

I almost laugh. "He didn't want me to pose naked or anything. I was just sitting in the kitchen doing homework."

Taylor unhooks the spiked collar around her throat and does a few neck rolls before refastening it. "But you flipped out anyway. Just like you did after the picnic the other night."

I take another gulp of coffee. "I smashed his camera, grabbed his keys off the counter and ripped out of the driveway in his car, not thinking about anything except finding the pictures."

"But you didn't find the pictures because you crashed his car instead. Sucks."

I pull another kitchen chair up to the table and sit down beside Taylor. "I was doing okay, you know—until a stupid cat ran out in front of me."

"Like it matters. You were doing okay this summer too—until your mom beat you to the buried treasure. That's what happened, right?"

"You know about that?" I groan.

Taylor gets up again to pour her own cup of coffee. "When I can't sleep at night, I sneak out and go swimming. Victoria would kill me if she knew, and my skin is probably radioactive now, but the water helps me relax." She leans against the counter and sips her evil brew. "This tastes like shit!" she exclaims, pouring the coffee down the sink and clomping back to sit beside me at the table. "Anyway, I was out about thirty feet from the dock last night when your mom and her posse were making to leave. Not wanting to be a party crasher, I thought it would be best to keep quiet and tread water. I didn't intentionally eavesdrop, and I didn't really hear anything, just some screeching by your mother and you running off with a box under your arm."

I can feel the red-hot glow of humiliation rising from my chin up and over my scalp.

"You don't have to be embarrassed, Sarah. It's not like your past comes as a huge shock to me anyway."

"Why's that?" I demand, except that I already know why. Taylor and I are just different breeds of the same species, like Great Danes and dachshunds. Despite our different looks and personalities, it didn't take either of us long to sniff out our similarities.

"The only difference between you and me," Taylor says, "is that I can't stand to be touched and you can't stand to be looked at. Now, which one of us would you rather be?"

Johanna sashays in just then through the porch door, wearing a shimmery halter and low-cut shorts so short that they must show off a good two inches of butt crack every time she bends to pick up poo. Nicholas and Brant trail her to the table, fighting over which of them she'll let rub sunblock onto her back today.

Taylor and I raise our eyebrows at each other. Neither of us would ever rather be Johanna.

"Hey, Hobbit," Brant calls out over our shoulders. "If you're just going to stand there by the fridge looking dopey, can you bring over the juice?"

"Hobbit" is what Brant calls Sullivan.

I slowly turn my head toward the refrigerator.

It's Sullivan all right, frozen in place. He must have gone upstairs for a shower after feeding the dogs and come in through the rec room. His hair is wet and his face is set in a scowl that I'm pretty sure indicates he's been standing there for a while.

I'm also pretty sure he's pissed off.

At me.

"Never mind, kid," Brant says when Sullivan ignores his juice request. "I'd rather have a beer anyway."

THIRTY

That ancient Montreal Expos pennant tacked to Sullivan's bedroom door drops off when he slams the door in my face. The gold tack lands by my foot. I wonder if I could hurt any worse than I already do if I slipped a sneaker off and stomped on the tack with my bare foot. I decide not to risk it. Running up here after him was stupid enough.

Down the hall, I hear the bathroom taps running full blast. I know Dr. Fred is still at the barn tending to a Yorkie's sore paw, and maybe, if I'm lucky, Victoria has her head under the tap, oblivious to the *BANG!* that just shook the lodge.

I rap on Sullivan's door.

Nothing.

My shaking hand grabs the knob and cracks open the door. Sullivan is sprawled out on his bottom bunk.

"What do you want?" he asks, staring straight up at his top bunk.

"I want to talk to you."

Sullivan sits up, his eyes shooting arrows through me. "You could have talked to me earlier."

"I didn't want to talk to anybody earlier."

Sullivan's wearing the black high-tops with yellow happy faces again, except the yellow grins seem to be leering at me this morning. "I asked you what happened with your mom, and you wouldn't tell me," he says. "But you go and tell Taylor a half hour later?"

"I didn't tell Taylor. She overheard my mom and me talking last night. I had to...clarify."

I'm not sure if Sullivan's even listening. His eyes are looking past me, as bright blue as ever, but angry as a hurricane. "You told her all that stuff about your past," he says. "About your dad. Is it even true?"

"I didn't tell her. She guessed most of it. I told you, I was just...clarifying."

"So it is true."

"Why the hell would I lie about something like that?" I say through clenched teeth.

"Why didn't you want me to know?" Sullivan demands.

"Why would I want anyone to know?" I shoot back.

"You just said Taylor knew."

"You're not listening!" I shout, sliding my back down Sullivan's door frame until I'm sitting cross-legged on his carpet. I push my hair out of my face and watch the wild storm raging in his eyes. "I said she guessed. And so did your mother, by the way. Victoria tried talking to me the day after the Dog Daze fiasco, but I kept quiet. If it were up to me, Sullivan, no one would ever have found out."

My voice breaks. "Except now, thanks to my mom and her stupid library fundraiser, the whole town of Riverwood probably knows. Are we broken up now?" I ask. Might as well get it over with now.

"Do you want to break up? Is that what you want?"

Be straight with him, that voice in my head asserts.

"Right now I...don't know what I want," I tell Sullivan. "At first I wasn't even sure I wanted to be with you—with anyone—because I knew that someday my...issues would cause problems." I laugh, a dark creepy laugh that tastes cold and sour in my mouth. "I just didn't realize how many problems. Or how soon they would happen. Or how much I'd really come to..."

Sullivan unties his high-tops and begins lacing them up again. "Your dad was...messing with you?"

I'm so tired of explaining. "Taking pictures. Naked photographs, Sullivan. Kiddie porn. For as long as I can remember. Until he died."

Sullivan looks like he's swallowed a bug. "And you couldn't stop him?"

My lips tremble, but I'm not going to start blubbering. "I didn't have a choice. It's not what you think. I—"

"Sometimes I just don't get you, Sarah."

Anger explodes like fireworks in my head. "You're right, Sullivan! You don't get me! You don't get that I didn't *let* my father take the pictures! He forced me! He threatened to kill my dog! You don't get how every click of my father's camera shutter felt like a bullet to my chest. You don't get that I know having pictures taken for school or the newspaper isn't the same thing. You don't get that I realize that the Dog Daze photographer meant no harm. You don't get that I understand why sometimes photographs are necessary. And you don't get that, despite all this knowing and understanding, that every click of any shutter—or even just having someone staring at me like you're doing now—even just blinking at me—still feels like…like…"

Taylor was right, I realize. My father was a rapist too. He raped me with his eyes.

Sullivan throws himself back on his bed.

With nothing left to lose, I continue to rant. "Before my mom turned up last night, I was going to ditch you at the concert next weekend and go looking for the Polaroids at the restaurant."

"Nice," Sullivan mumbles.

I take a deep breath. "But my mom found the pictures yesterday."

Silence from Sullivan.

"I burned them at the beach last night."

"That must be a relief."

"It's not, Sullivan! The pictures are gone, and that's a relief, for sure. But the shame and the guilt and the memories are still with me, just like a big, stinking, moldy pot of…leftovers."

And you aren't helping matters by copping an attitude with me, I think, blinking back hot tears.

He rises up on an elbow and stares me down again. "What are you going to do about them?"

"About what?"

"The leftovers."

"What everyone does with leftovers, Sullivan. Shove them to the back of the fridge and hopefully forget they exist."

"For how long?"

"Forever."

After a long silence, I dare to rise from the floor and plunk myself down next to Sullivan on the bottom bunk.

Another long silence.

"Are we still on for the concert?" I ask.

Sullivan ignores my question. He grinds his teeth and stares down at his knuckles.

I put my hand on his arm. He doesn't pull away, but he flinches, so I let go.

"Last night," he starts, his voice husky, "I thought I had a girlfriend. Not just a girlfriend, but a real friend-friend, you know? One who didn't mind that I was too short, or that I talked too much, or that my mother's a bit...over-involved...in my life. One who was so nice that she gave up all her spare time—for weeks—to help me out with the dog puzzle."

I sit there chewing on my thumb, feeling like a heel.

"But it turns out that you were only using me so I'd take you to the city." He pauses to wipe his nose on the back of his hand. "So you could ditch me."

"I would have helped you with the puzzle anyway." I'd like to think that's true, even though it's too late now to know for sure. "And I never wanted to ditch you.

I thought it was my only option. I thought finding and destroying those pictures would help me move on. I just thought it might make me not so...so weird...about stuff."

"I never minded that you were weird."

"You would have eventually," I retort.

"You don't know that!"

"I'm sorry, Sullivan." I get up to leave. I don't know what else to say. I know I shouldn't expect his forgiveness. I knew all along that using him was terrible. I knew all along that the story of Sarah and Sullivan would never end with fireworks and a Ferris-wheel kiss.

So why does it feel that my heart has been ripped out by pit bulls?

I'm halfway down the hall when I hear "Sarah?"

I backtrack and pause by his door. The anger has drained from his face. Sullivan is pale now. Hurt. Sad.

This truth takes about ten seconds to hit me. And when it does, it tramples me and pins me to the floor, not unlike Judy did that first day in the kitchen.

Sullivan has leftovers too, and they aren't just the big feet and the kidney and liver problems and that other stuff Victoria blabbed to me about that day in my cabin—the physical aftereffects of his cancer. Sullivan hasn't once, all summer, talked about the future—where he wants to go to university or what career path he wants to pursue. He rushes from activity to activity at school, from crowd to crowd, like he wants to make sure he tries everything, and meets everyone, at least once. He goes along with his mother's over-zealous rules about rain gear and sunblock and bedtime.

Sullivan's leftovers are even worse than my leftovers. My father is dead. He's never coming back. Sullivan's cancer can come back anytime.

I walk over to the bed and sit down next to Sullivan, half expecting that he'll push me away. But he doesn't. We just sit quietly for a few minutes, not saying anything, not doing anything.

"Does this mean we're still on for pizza before the concert?" he asks eventually.

I lean back and raise an eyebrow at him. "It depends. Are you a black olive guy or a green olive guy? Because it matters."

Sullivan grabs my hand, intertwining his fingers in mine. "Sarah, I'm sorry. I said you could trust me and then I flip out just because Taylor found out first. I know you had your...reasons. I can imagine how hard it must—"

"Hey! Focus! Black olives or green olives?"

Sullivan leans forward. He kisses me long and hard, a kiss that feels different from all his previous kisses.

I'd like to think it's a kiss with a future.

"Green. Definitely green, Sarah Greene," he replies eventually, his voice garbled because his tongue is still in my mouth.

"Then it's a date," I confirm.

Sullivan sits back. He's got spit on his lip. His or mine, who knows. "Sarah?"

"Yeah?"

"You don't really like Ratgut, do you?"

"Um...no. But I do really like the guy I'm going with."

THIRTY-ONE

An hour later, I tap on the open door of Dr. Fred's office.

Johanna, Taylor, Brant, Nicholas and I are all being summoned, one at a time, for what he calls our "mid-summer evaluations."

"Sarah!" Dr. Fred exclaims. He flashes me a big toothy grin and waves me in as if he hasn't seen me in months.

I scan his desk for signs of report cards, ranking sheets, papers with check boxes ranging from poor to excellent—typical evaluation stuff—but there are none. The desk is bare, as bald and shiny as the top of Dr. Fred's head.

"Have a seat," he says, gesturing me into a rusty lawn chair he's set up across from his desk. Then he reaches into a desk drawer, pulls out a bag of red licorice twists and pushes it toward me. I shake my head; I'm so nervous I'd probably choke. Dr. Fred extracts a strand from the package and chomps down on it.

"Sarah, Sarah, Sarah." Dr. Fred swallows and leans back in his chair. A red licorice blob is stuck between his bottom teeth. "I want you to know that you're doing a spectacular job this summer. Just marvellous!"

"Uh…thanks."

"I don't think we've ever had a volunteer like you before. So eager. So dedicated to really making the very most of your time here. Your work with the dogs is fantastic. And that lasagna you served last night was the tastiest thing I've ever eaten." He lowers his voice. "I dread going back to Victoria's Thursday-night meatloaf in September."

"Um…thanks." Am I in the running for some bizarre "Young Offender of the Year" award?

"I wanted to ask you a serious question," Dr. Fred continues. "Have you ever considered becoming a—"

"A chef? I can't say I'd rather clean toilets for a living, but—"

"No, no—though you'd be a great one. And I do hope your biscuit recipes turn into the best-selling dog treats of all time. But what I was going to ask is, have you ever considered becoming a veterinarian?"

"Wow…I…well…you really think I could do that?"

"Absolutely!" He folds up the bag of licorice and tosses it back in the drawer. "How are you at science?"

"Good enough, I guess."

Ha. I'm great at science. I'm not super smart, and I've never been especially driven to do well at school. But years of using homework as an excuse to avoid my father has left me with excellent study skills.

"Wonderful!" Dr. Fred beams. "If you ever need anything, Sarah, just come to me. A reference for school.

Advice on which courses to take. A student placement. Seriously, I'm happy to help any way I can. I guess you've already got, as we say here at Camp Dog Gone Fun, a leg up in a pet nutrition specialty. And with Judy—it's like… you've got magic. I was so afraid that Judy would never be able to bond with anyone, to trust anyone again. You've made me think she might be adoptable after all."

Bond? Trust? I don't like the sound of that. Until now, I've just pegged Judy as someone's birthday or Christmas puppy. A cute and adorable puppy who quickly morphed into an obnoxious and overwhelming puppy. Too much of a good thing. The big hairy gift that kept on giving and giving and giving. I saw Judy's owners getting exhausted and putting her out with the other party trash.

"Why did Judy end up at the shelter?" I ask Dr. Fred.

Dr. Fred points at the wall behind my left shoulder. I swivel in my chair. All I see is a calendar. A typical "puppy in a picnic basket" photo above the date squares. (Date squares? Maybe dessert on Saturday?) I'd seen the calendar many times before when I'd come into Dr. Fred's office on quests for paper clips or pens, but it never clicked that the cute black puppy with the pink ribbon around its neck could actually be Judy. I'd even seen that same puppy photo on binders and journal covers.

Was Judy really ever small enough to fit inside a picnic basket?

"Judy was owned by the Redmores," Dr. Fred says. "Of the CTA, Canine Talent Agency. They're based not far from here, near Prescott."

"Never heard of them."

"The Redmores also owned a golden retriever who starred in a series of heartworm medication commercials. And a trio of standard poodles. Bella, Stella and the Fella starred in that silly *Happy Hot Dog* movie. You've seen it?"

I shake my head. "The Redmores wanted to turn Judy into a movie star?"

Dr. Fred shrugs. "Judy loves to be the center of attention. They thought she'd be a natural at it. They might even have settled for print ads, calendars and greeting cards...but..."

My stomach knows where this conversation is going before my brain does. Without warning, my breakfast cereal works its way up my throat. Fruit chunks threaten to fly out of my mouth. I swallow hard.

"But you know Judy, Sarah," Dr. Fred continues. "She won't stay still. And that adorable twenty-pound puppy she was in that photograph quickly grew into a huge, athletic dog who needs more exercise every day than most dogs need in a month. She's so high-spirited and impulsive and easily distracted that—you know this better than anyone— she's very hard to train."

"She wouldn't sit still for the camera," I say slowly, unable to keep an angry quiver out of my voice. "She didn't like the ribbons and hats and...props." I suck in my breath, not sure if I want to let it back out. "Did they beat her?" I ask finally.

Dr. Fred sighs. "I suppose when the usual treats and praise wouldn't keep her still, they began using some more...coercive techniques."

"And when that wouldn't work?" In my mind, I've left Dr. Fred's office; I'm back in my father's restaurant's storeroom, my face red with fury and humiliation, my eyes dark and hostile, goose bumps all over.

It's true that my father never laid a hand on me, ever. Instead he coerced me with threats. All so I would do his bidding. I hated him—and myself—a little more each time.

Dr. Fred frowns. "Her constant whining and howling annoyed the neighbors, who, thank God, contacted the police, who contacted me. I respond to all animal abuse calls for the region."

Just hearing the words "animal abuse" makes my stomach feel like it's being forced through a juicer. Then again, maybe it's helping abused and hurt and sick animals that makes Dr. Fred so happy all the time.

Dr. Fred continues. "My assistant and I traveled up to the Redmores' in June, the weekend before Canada Day. We didn't even have to gain entry to the house. There was poor Judy, shaking and howling, chained to a cement post in the garage-turned-photo-studio. Her face was covered in dried blood. Across the floor was an upended tripod. Mr. Redmore was so arrogant that he actually admitted he'd taken a swing at 'that bloody stupid mutt' with it. Thought it would 'knock some sense into her.'"

My eyes are on fire. Then they flood.

Dr. Fred rushes around from the other side of his desk. Lays a hand on my shoulder. "Sarah, Sarah, don't cry. We shut them down! The Redmores can't own or work with animals ever again. And we took Judy into care. She healed—

physically anyway—well ahead of schedule. At first I wasn't sure about my decision to bring her over here to the island. I thought it might be too soon to integrate her into the general shelter population. But now I'm so glad I did. You've been wonderful with her!"

My head snaps up. Suddenly, something makes perfect sense to me. I wipe my eyes on my shirtsleeve and look Dr. Fred right in the eye. "Judy's not afraid of thunderstorms," I gasp.

He goes back around his desk and sits down, looking a little puzzled.

"It's not the thunder," I say. "Or even the lightning. Not really. It's the flash."

Dr. Fred scratches his chin.

"The flash reminds Judy of the camera. You know that night at the Dog Daze Festival? The photographer was taking flash pictures."

Dr. Fred picks up my train of thought. "I think you're on to something, Sarah."

I can't answer. I can't even nod. I just sniff again, biting my lip, trying not to bawl, to draw even more attention to myself.

Just the way Taylor and I had recognized each other for what we are, Judy had me pegged from that first day, when she charged through the kitchen and nailed me to the floor with those big slurpy kisses.

Judy has leftovers too.

Only in her case, they'd be called a doggy bag.

Dr. Fred looks frantically around his office. He runs over to a shelf and returns to my side with a box of Kleenex.

"Sarah, Sarah, what's wrong?" he asks. "Judy will be fine, especially with you here to help her. Sarah? Should I call Victoria? Would you like a drink of water?"

"I'm okay," I croak. "Can I go now?"

Dr. Fred rubs the bridge of his nose as I rise and make a beeline for the office door. "Well, if you're sure. I don't want..." He reaches back into his desk drawer. "Are you sure you wouldn't like some candy?"

"I'm fine. I...I should be starting lunch," I explain, backing out the office doorway before Dr. Fred can change his mind.

Two steps out the door, I stop in my tracks. I step back into the office. "Dr. Fred?"

"Yes, Sarah."

"Judy's coming home with me at the end of the summer. I'll adopt her. I know Mom won't mind." I don't know anything of the sort, but she owes me.

Dr. Fred grins. "I was hoping you'd say that."

THIRTY-TWO

Grrrrr. September.

Composting leftovers isn't an overnight fix. I haven't
suddenly moved to la-la land. But it's fair to say that things
are moving forward.

School starts on a hot and rainy Tuesday. I've had my
hair cut and it feels frizzy. My jeans are stuck to my legs
with sweat. I've just walked into my first class to discover
I've landed Doris the Demented for grade twelve homeroom and that the school computer has scheduled me for
chemistry, physics, algebra and bio, all in the first semester,
boom, boom, boom, boom.

Nothing has changed in the seat behind me: Jeff
Grenville is still drumming Pink Floyd and Def Leppard
anthems on his desktop with his thumbs.

Sullivan is two seats up on the right, bent over his
class schedule, while Doris the Demented copies down the
seating plan. He has art, gym, medieval history and drama
this semester.

"You big suck," I said to him earlier, when we were assigned our lockers.

"Big and tall suck," he laughed, puffing out his chest.

It's true: Sullivan is starting to look too big for his desk, the way the other seventeen-year-old guys in class do. He went to the doctor last week for his annual checkup and found out that a) he's still cancer-free and b) he's grown three inches over the summer. This was confirmed a few days ago when we ran into Brant at Riverwood Plaza. He was in town visiting a relative.

"Hey!" Brant bounded across the restaurant to Sullivan and me. "It's Chef Boyar-Dog Biscuit and her boyfriend." He sized Sullivan up. "I think you've grown, Stretch. You're almost tall enough now to sniff my pits."

Anyhow, Victoria thinks Sullivan's first growth spurt in four years is a fluke—or a miracle.

Please. It's my cooking.

Back in Doris the Demented's class, Sullivan swivels in his desk every few minutes and grins at me in a way that makes me want to melt into the floor and laugh out loud at the same time. But when I see him scrawl his name on the attendance sheet that's being passed around, my jaw drops onto my desk. Then again, I should have known.

"Hey! Sullivan!" I whisper up to him.

"Hi!" He turns and waves.

"You're left-handed!" It's amazing the things I've been noticing now that Sullivan's crazy shoes, and my own scared and scheming reflection in his eyes, are no longer distracting me from who he really is.

"Cool, man! So was Jimi Hendrix," Jeff pipes up from behind me, giving Sullivan an impressed nod over my shoulder.

I swear Sullivan will grow another inch by tomorrow just from having the most hard-core dude in our school call him "man."

At lunch, he and I walk the few blocks to my house to feed Judy—and ourselves—and to toss a Frisbee around in the backyard. My mother doesn't leave for work until after 2:00 PM, so there will be no making out.

Not that Sullivan and I will ever become one of those school couples who spend every spare second between classes grabbing each other's asses and sucking each other's tongues. Because, face it, I'll never be an exhibitionist. Starting next week, Sullivan has volleyball practice and musical auditions and the multicultural festival and God-knows-what-else to work on at lunch and after school.

Just so I don't end up sitting alone in the library, reading paperbacks, while Sullivan is out scratching a dozen items off his life's to-do list every hour (as long as he doesn't start adding other girls' names to that to-do list, I'm fine with it), I let myself be coerced by Sullivan's father—advisor to all non-sporting, non-arts extracurriculars—to lead this year's cooking club.

"I hear you're a wonderful cook, Sarah." Mr. Vickerson corners me outside the bio lab before period four.

"Uh...I mostly bake dog biscuits these days."

"That's too bad. The cooking club cooks for charity. Bake sales, pizzas, stuff like that."

"Which charity?"

"You get to decide."

"Camp Dog Gone Fun?" I blurt out before remembering that Dr. Fred is the reason Mr. Vickerson is divorced.

He shrugs. "Fine by me."

My brain flashes to a poster tacked onto a bathroom wall in the city the night Sullivan and I went to the Ratgut concert.

"Or how about using some of the money to raise awareness around school about the Kids Help Phone?" I suggest. Because, face it, not every kid's "Uncle Joe" dies like mine did. Most kids need more than a stroke of luck to make the abuse stop.

"Wonderful idea!" Mr. Vickerson says, tapping a pen against his clipboard. "So I can mark you down?"

"Sure, but no yearbook photos, okay?"

I'm not sure how much he knows about me, but it's enough for him to say, "Not if you don't want one."

"I don't."

"Maybe you'll change your mind."

Don't hold your breath. Then again, now that my father's despicable Polaroids are gone, my life seems more open-ended. The possibility of me changing my mind about photography isn't necessarily a given, but it is an option.

"Maybe," I say as I take a step toward class. All I need on Day One is a detention for being late.

"Oh, Sarah?" Mr. Vickerson is rooting around in the canvas briefcase he carries between classes. He extracts a small paper bag. "Pass this on to Sullivan when you see him."

"Will do," I choke, stuffing the paper bag into my backpack and running into bio while Mr. Vickerson stands there chuckling.

I'm pretty sure it's condoms in the bag. Mr. Vickerson has given Sullivan eleven boxes since he arrived home from Moose Island and broke the news to his father that I am his girlfriend. Sullivan hasn't bothered telling his dad that we aren't actually having sex yet—he still has all the condoms Brant gave him too—because he's hoping that we will be sooner rather than later.

Sullivan laughed last night when I was over at his house while Mr. Vickerson attended a school board meeting. "Sarah, don't you know what a tragedy it will be if I survive cancer only to die of sexual frustration?"

Doesn't he get what a big step it is for me just to slide into third base by candlelight?

Sullivan does get it. Mostly. A typical pre–make-out conversation goes like this:

"One candle, Sullivan. Not fifteen!"

"Ten?"

"Two."

"Seven?"

"Two. Final answer."

A few days ago, with a written recommendation from Dr. Fred in my hand, I walked across town with Judy to offer my services at the local veterinary clinic. I want to volunteer behind the scenes: taking the boarded dogs for walks, playing with kittens, talking to parrots. I want to get a feel for the everyday workings of an animal hospital, to see if I've really got the guts to work with animals for a living.

Turns out that one of the hospital's weekend receptionists left last week to go back to university. Pre-vet at Guelph. Given my experience at Camp Dog Gone Fun and my glowing reference from Dr. Fred, they hired me on the spot to replace her. And I get paid! Not much, but it'll be nice to give up my shifts at Doughy Donuts and still have some cash on hand to go out with Sullivan *and* buy ingredients for my dog biscuit experiments. (My mother made me put the promised payment from Helen at Tricks for Treats, Inc., straight into my university fund. Boring, but necessary, since my father's restaurant is finally on the market, but so far no takers. Bad karma, you think?)

I make a huge spaghetti dinner for my mother and Tanner to celebrate Tanner's popping of the big question last weekend. Mom said yes.

Thank God or Matthew McConaughey, because planning her wedding takes her mind off me. After I came home from Camp Dog Gone Fun, I'd hear her roaming the house late at night, mumbling to herself, asking the furniture and the walls if I will ever forgive her for not seeing through my father, oblivious to the fact I already have forgiven her. (At least that's what I tell her. And myself.) She also worries out loud about Sullivan and me. About whether one of us will get hurt when it's time to leave for university. About whether she should do something about us spending so much time up in my room after dark. About whether she should be grateful that I'm not like those girls she saw on Dr. Phil a few weeks back, out walking the streets in fishnets, spreading their legs for crack.

"Sarah?" Mom says, wiping her mouth on a napkin.

"Yeah."

"This sauce is even better than...well, let's just say it's the best sauce I've ever eaten."

Yay, Mom. There will be no leftovers tonight.

Tanner seconds the motion, pushes back his chair and carries his empty plate to the dishwasher. His days of eating Hungry Man dinners are so over.

"You ready?" he asks me.

Tanner, of all people, is teaching me to drive. He takes me to the Canadian Tire parking lot after hours to practice. Judy comes along on these test drives—somehow her hot breath in my ear as she hangs her big hairy head over the back of the driver's seat is reassuring, not distracting. Tanner doesn't complain about the doggy smell or hairs in the backseat of his new car. As far as I can tell, his only problem with Judy is her insistence on licking his face every time she sees him.

Tanner never asks when I'm going for my license. He knows it's not about the driving for me. It's about the photo ID. But it's nice to know that he's making sure I'll pass when and if the time is ever right. (Or, at the very least, if I'm ever tempted to steal his car again, I won't crash it.)

He says if I ever change my mind about working at the clinic or writing cookbooks, I can come work for him at Canadian Tire.

"You think I have an aptitude for selling gardening tools and plumbing supplies?" I ask.

"I think you have an aptitude for whatever you set your mind to, Sarah."

Tomorrow is picture day, I remember as I reach over Judy's bulk to switch off my bedside lamp. (Our sleepovers are nightly now. I need a bigger bed.)

Mom says that I don't have to show up to school in the morning. That I don't have to sit for a picture just to prove to her or Sullivan or anyone else that I'm okay now.

Because chances are I'm not okay. Not yet. Maybe I'll never be able to "Say cheese!" Maybe it will have to be enough that I make a fantastic three-cheese omelet.

But I'm going to show up to school and try it anyway, and just hope that I don't upend any tripods. I'm going to wear my unofficial Camp Dog Gone Fun sweatshirt, the one that Judy and the other dogs walked over with paint-covered paws on everyone's last day on Moose Island. It's not really classy. The Riverwood High School fashion police will be on high alert.

But I'm thinking it will boost my courage. I never had the courage to tell anyone about my father and the Polaroids, but I'll do whatever it takes to find the courage to move forward with my life.

I know I shouldn't recommend unlawful behavior as a way to get ahead, but, well…it worked for me. Moose Island is where I got what we at Camp Dog Gone Fun call a new leash on life.

ACKNOWLEDGMENTS

Many thanks to Sarah Harvey and the rest of the wonderful team at Orca, whose expertise brought this book to life.

Heather Waldorf was born in Ottawa and raised in small-town eastern Ontario. She now lives in Toronto with Moose, a twelve-year-old golden retriever. Heather is addicted to green tea, jigsaw puzzles, mystery novels and the TV show *Bones*. Also a lover of the great outdoors, she's never written a novel that doesn't, at some point, put the main character in a canoe. Her previous novels for teens include *Fighting the Current*, *Grist* and *Tripping*.